Shelley Stoehr

Tomorrow Wendy

A Love Story

DELACORTE PRESS

Published by
Delacorte Press
Bantam Doubleday Dell Publishing Group, Inc.
1540 Broadway
New York, New York 10036

Library of Congress Cataloging-in-Publication Data
Stoehr, Shelley.
     Tomorrow Wendy : a love story / Shelley Stoehr.
          p.   cm.
     Summary: Seventeen-year-old Cary seems to have
it all—cool boyfriend, wealthy family, and a great
sense of style, but she also has a serious problem.
     ISBN 0-385-32339-5
     [1. Lesbians—Fiction.   2. Interpersonal
relations—Fiction.]   I. Title.
     PZ7.S8695To   1998
     [Fic]—dc21   97-24547
                                                      CIP
                                                       AC

Book design by Semadar Megged
Manufactured in the United States of America
March 1998
10   9   8   7   6   5   4   3   2   1
BVG

This book is dedicated to everyone
who's ever risked falling in,
or out of, love.

Chapter

1

"ARE YOU A UNICORN / OR ARE YOU JUST HAPPY TO SEE *me?"* he said as I passed him, heading up the school steps.

He was tall and thin, and glittery around the edges. I'd never seen him before, but I knew his name, and it was like I'd always known him. Adjusting my wide-brimmed Audrey Hepburn hat, I pulled open the front door wide enough so that he and his beaten old nylon-stringed guitar could fit through, too.

"You're Rad, aren't you?" I said.

He nodded, tugging at the twisted red bandanna he wore knotted around his neck, like it was keeping his head on or something. Inside the building he didn't glitter as much as in the morning fall sunlight, but still there was something. Like his cropped hair was too blond to really be there, and the bristly goatee definitely didn't fit at Babylon High.

Tugging at his long flannel sleeves, which hung past his fingertips, he said, *"I'm a little bit country / I'm a little bit rock and roll."*

1

"I know you," I said. "How come you always talk in song lyrics?"

He shrugged, saying, *"Every sentence in my head / Someone else has said,"* and followed me into the cafeteria. People moved around him and didn't acknowledge him. But not that many people paid attention to me, either.

"We're going to be friends, aren't we?" I said as he walked away, the guitar swinging and banging against his side.

"You've got a friend in need," he sang.

I took that to be a yes.

"Cary!" my boyfriend, Danny, yelled from across the cafeteria. "Over here!"

I turned to look, and waved. Turning back to Rad, I was going to ask him to come sit at our table, but he was gone. That was when I knew this year was going to be different. Things were going to happen fast, and weird, and not at all like in an Audrey Hepburn movie.

Chapter

2

Danny walked me to my first-period class, calculus. He had my left hand, and I held up my long skirt slightly with my free hand so I wouldn't trip. My mother once said I had delicate features, like Audrey Hepburn, and the first time I saw *Breakfast at Tiffany's* I was so in love with her I decided to complete the picture. I dress like Audrey, and I wear my hair in Hepburn styles, usually pinned up on top of my head with little brunette wisps brushing over my eyelashes. And now my mother wishes she'd kept her mouth shut.

She tries to make me watch *Beverly Hills 90210* and buys me really expensive little cropped shirts and shiny miniskirts, but I don't wear them. Those outfits aren't even stylish here anyway. This is New York, not California! Babylon is as different from Beverly Hills as you can probably get. There's some grunge, but mostly kids are into the gangsta look, especially the white kids. Then there are the standard, don't-get-in-anyone's-face preppies. And lurking in the bathroom corners are the throwbacks to the subur-

3

ban dirtbag-metalheads who wear holey jeans and old Metallica T-shirts handed down from older siblings.

Still, as eclectic as the styles are, I am alone in my dead-movie-star look, which is the way I like it. It gets me noticed, but it also keeps people from looking too closely. I've discovered that if you wear a big enough hat, no one worries much about what's going on inside your head. Anyway, the Audrey look means that now I'm not usually allowed to go to the country club with Mom and Dad, since I might embarrass them. Which is fine with me. I mean, they won't let me drink, and it's not like there are any good drugs there.

Danny can always find the best drugs. He lives just off Cooper Street, which is kind of the poor section of town. But it's also where some of the coolest kids live, the ones who shop the thrift shops like me, even though I don't really have to. Danny even has an earring. His head is shaved on the sides, and his black hair is long in the back, usually tied in a ponytail. A lot of girls think he's really hot. I don't know about that, but I like being around him. We always do fun stuff, and he doesn't mind that I dress so retro-weird. I only want to *look* like Audrey Hepburn, I don't want to *be* her, all sweet and shit. Not around here. I'd never survive.

• • •

Just as the bell rang for first period, Danny kissed me goodbye, and I hurried into the classroom to my seat. I looked for her, two rows ahead of me and one seat to the left. She was late, or maybe she wasn't coming in today. I should've asked Danny before—Wendy's his twin sister.

"Cary," Mr. Curry said from the front of the room, "take off the hat. No hats in class."

I sighed, and someone snickered. It was a brand-new hat, and I was hoping Wendy would get to see it on me. I was always trying to get her to notice me, but even though I'd been going out with Danny for almost a year, she mostly looked right through me. Of course, she was always high, so I didn't take it too personally. Besides, for twins she and Danny were unusual—they hardly ever got along. For a while I'd been waiting for the sibling love to set in, and hoping it would extend to me. I mean, Danny likes me so much—why can't Wendy?

I actually saw Wendy first. Before I started going out with Danny last school year, I used to hang around Wendy's locker. I could never figure out how to talk to her. She was dangerous and aloof, and so beautiful in a sunken-eyed, sad way. But sad in a self-absorbed way. Wendy didn't seem to care about anything. Her expression was a big "fuck you," and she didn't need to hide under hats.

I think my crush started after I realized I couldn't actually be her; the best I could hope for was to be with her. After I chickened out on making that happen, I ended up with Danny. Now I love him, too, and I wonder sometimes if I even know what love is. All my feelings seem real, yet I can't commit to one set of emotions. For now, I go out with Danny and worship Wendy quietly, still trying to figure out how to talk to her. It's like I can never do anything directly. It has to be a puzzle or in code or something.

Which is why I like calculus, and why I took my hat off

right away, without arguing. Mr. Curry's pretty cool. Still, I couldn't help being a little angry because I might have hat-head.

As I scrunched the hair on top of my head so it would fluff out into a poofy ball, and checked that the bobby pins were secure, Wendy shuffled in. She dumped her thick calc. book on her desk and slid into her seat, which didn't look easy. Her pink dress was as tight as a condom on an erection. Even with her short green hair—what the upper-middle-class white snoots around here would normally shun—Wendy was very popular. It probably had a lot to do with her bigger-than-average breasts, and the way she didn't really walk, she sort of swung, like her hips floated from a private pendulum. I tried to walk like her once and I tripped over myself and fell. Maybe if I smoked more pot, I could do it. But I'm pretty sure I'd still only hurt myself.

"Late pass, Wendy?" Mr. Curry asked.

Wendy pushed herself slowly out of her chair and brought a pink slip to the front. I tried not to let anyone see that I was staring at her ass and finally had to look down at my notebook so I wouldn't blush.

• • •

As I left calculus, I put my new hat back on and waited by the door for Wendy, inconspicuously, I hoped. "Hi," I said as she sashayed past me.

"Uh-huh" was all she said as she continued down the hall.

I watched her for a second, then lifted my skirt a little, adjusted the strap of my book bag, and headed toward my next class, French. It was on the third floor and not easy to get to in the three minutes between bells. It would be

6

harder now that I'd wasted time waiting for Wendy. Sometimes I can be so stupid it hurts.

At the second-floor landing, which was deserted because the bell was about to ring and everyone was already where they should be, I bumped into the neck of a guitar. It twanged, and I smiled at my new friend Rad as he jogged with me up the last flight of stairs.

"Do you think it's crazy to love your boyfriend's sister?" I asked as we got close to the top.

His fingers poked out from his long flannel sleeve and strummed a quick chord. *"It's easier not to be wise / And measure these things with your brains,"* he said.

"Do you always have to be so cryptic, or do you want to tell me what you mean?"

"Measure in love," he said.

"I wish I could," I said. "But I can't even talk to her."

The bell rang as Rad waved his hand to shush me.

"Words are very unnecessary / They can only do harm," he said.

And then he was gone, and I had to switch my brain from songs to French, the language of lovers. Rad seemed to get whatever I was feeling, even if I didn't, like when you listen to the radio and the songs seem to be all about *you*. Except Rad was more real. As real as all my messed up feelings, and just as hard to figure out.

I hoped he'd start giving me some clear answers, soon. Because here I was, in love with two people. And not just any two people, but two people who came from the same womb. And only one had a dick, which made everything more confusing. Thank God it was Friday.

Chapter

3

After school Danny met me at my locker. When he kissed me, I grimaced a little because his face was bristly and burned my cheek. I tried not to stiffen too much and followed him outside, my book bag heavy with weekend homework. Danny carried only a spiral-bound notebook with a pen stuck in the metal loops. I knew there were no words inside, only pictures—the scratchy doodles that he said kept him from going crazy. He never studied, or took notes, or anything. But he was some kind of genius and always did better than me in school. The reason he wasn't in advanced calculus with Wendy and me was because he took it last year, as a junior. He'd probably be valedictorian this year, which will make my mother want to puke and my father shake his head and sigh with disappointment. You'd think they'd be glad I have a smart boyfriend, but no. They want *me* to be first. Which isn't going to happen. I'm smart, and I do well in school, but I don't care that much about grades lately. I've got a lot more on my mind.

The book bag strap dug into my shoulder, even through the fake-leopard jacket I wore. Danny and I were headed for the bleachers near the football field. Shivering, I rubbed my hands and the parts of my arms that weren't covered by the three-quarter sleeves of my jacket. The tiny collar didn't protect my neck much from the wind that skittered in from Argyle Lake, and I almost lost my hat in one fierce gust. I don't know why the cold didn't bother Danny. He was wearing a leather jacket, but only thermal underwear under a pair of torn Bermuda shorts.

Although I was freezing, I followed Danny under the bleachers because he was, after all, my boyfriend. Last spring I even liked these after-school meetings with Danny's friends. But it was warmer then. By the time the joint was passed to me, my hands were almost too cold to hold it. If I hadn't already known I was going to Danny's house after, I wouldn't have bothered to smoke at all.

After a few more hits, I felt better. It was still cold, and getting colder, but the colored leaves lying around the lake looked pretty in the fading sunlight, and they even covered the duck and goose turds. When Danny pulled me close, I sank into his warmth.

"Phantasie tonight?" Danny's friend Brian said.

Phantasie was the coolest underage dance club on Long Island. They played decent music, and it was easy to sneak in liquor, so we spent a lot of time there.

"Right on," said Danny, high-fiving.

"Who's got some E?"

"I got coke."

"Nah, they've been checking the bathrooms, even frisking some dudes at the door. Ralph got busted last week. I don't want to get caught carrying."

"You think Big Joe's working the door tonight? Maybe he could score some E for us."

Danny waved his hand in front of his face and shook his head. "I got it covered. Don't worry about it. Twenty a hit, okay?"

"Cool. Parking lot, ten o'clock?"

"Eleven."

"Oh man, Danny, I gotta be home by one . . ."

"Fuck that. Eleven o'clock."

The kid looked so geeky with his little zits glowing red in the failing sunlight, I almost laughed when he sighed and scraped his foot in the dirt, pouting. Danny was so cool. These guys would lick his Doc Martens if he asked them, and they'd like it, too.

"Later," Danny said, waving and leading me out from under the bleachers. He must've been really high, because he took my book bag and carried it for me, all the way to his house.

• • •

There was no one home at Danny's when we got there. There almost never was. Both his parents worked. Which was convenient for Danny, since he only had me over for sex.

I stepped over the broken top step, but Danny put his foot right onto the rotting and cracked wood. I cringed as his foot sank in a little too far. I was always sure he'd go right through and break his leg, but of course he bounced right up onto the porch next to me.

"Someone should fix that step," I said inside, rubbing my hands.

He shrugged. "I guess, maybe. You want something to drink?"

I nodded as he began flicking on lights so we wouldn't trip over the newspapers and clothes and stuff on the floor. Danny filled up two Burger King/Disney glasses, half with vodka from a big plastic bottle and half with orange juice. Drinking quickly, we headed up the stairs to his room. While Danny smoked a cigarette at his dresser and combed his ponytail, I took off my stockings. If I let him do it, he'd rip them. His fingernails were longer than mine.

• • •

Without even trying, Danny really did have a great body. I was thinking that as he lay on top of me, naked. I liked lying with him in the late afternoons after getting high, smelling the shampoo scent of his soft black hair. Little bones in his shoulders gave way to ropy thin muscles that were almost feminine. His hands were gentle, and his lips were soft. He never rushed into sex like the other guys I'd slept with. The country club guys were always in a hurry because they were always afraid of being caught. But since Danny's parents didn't get home until late, it wasn't a problem for us. Anyway, no one ever caught Danny doing anything.

My eyes were shut, and I was zoning out and just beginning to enjoy Danny's fingertips on my nipples when he asked, "You want me to get Wendy's vibrator? She has one. I know where she keeps it."

Her name from his mouth gave me a little chill and totally threw me off. Opening my eyes, I half expected him to be leering, like he'd said it on purpose to screw with my head. But he was smiling softly and seriously, just being Danny, trying to think of everything. So I shook my head, and we kissed some more. Sloppy, wet kisses that left drool in the corners of my mouth. After all this time I still didn't know what to do about the drool thing. I mean, was it rude to wipe it away?

Now my concentration was totally gone, and I began to wish Danny would stop being so fucking "considerate" and just do it already.

"Can I?" I asked, fiddling with his ponytail.

He nodded, and I gently let his hair down so it fell over me like a veil and I could lose myself in the smell while Danny slid on a condom.

• • •

One of the things that I liked best about Danny in bed was that he always wore a condom. It wasn't because I was afraid of getting pregnant, because I was on the pill. It wasn't because I was afraid of AIDS. I don't know, but I always felt like that was the least of my worries when I was having sex with a guy. I was more worried he'd notice I wasn't that turned on and think there was something wrong with me, which maybe there was. With a lubricated condom, he couldn't tell if I liked it or not, and that was a relief.

• • •

Danny always came like it was the last thing he was going to do in this lifetime. It sent a tingle up my spine even when I wasn't actually coming myself, which was always. Rolling off me, he kissed me on the forehead and closed his eyes.

"See you tonight," I whispered, getting up.

"Uh-huh," he said, already half-asleep. "Pick you up at ten."

"Cool," I said.

• • •

Danny was snoring by the time I was dressed. I turned off his light as I slipped out into the hall, carrying my shoes in my hand.

There still wasn't anyone home, but even so, I tiptoed down the hall to Wendy's room. My scalp tingled as I opened the door. There was always the chance she might be home, in there sleeping. Or she could come home and catch me touching her stuff. She'd kill me, I was pretty sure. But sneaking into her space was as much a ritual for me as going to sleep after sex was for Danny. I couldn't go home until I'd stolen a souvenir.

First I smelled her pillow, which had a greenish tint from where her hair color had worn off. It smelled vaguely like pot, a little like dirt, and a lot like cat hair. I knew there was a cat somewhere in the room, but it never came out unless Wendy was there. Danny said his parents didn't even know she had a cat.

Her hairbrush was on the dresser, but I already had lots of her hair in my collection. Opening the closet door, I cringed when it creaked and held my breath for a second. The house was quiet, and I started pushing through the clothes, which were few—most of Wendy's stuff was on the floor, or on the back of her desk chair, or on the bed in a heap. I found what I was looking for—a big, long-haired cardigan, like something Kurt Cobain used to wear. Carefully I plucked some of the sweater-fur from the armpit and held it tightly between my fingertips all the way downstairs. I put it in my wallet and let myself out.

Rocking on the broken top step was Rad. He scared the crap out of me, and I almost fell.

"They'll only give you what you're taking," he said, pulling at his goatee, and nodding at my purse, like he knew what was inside.

I was big-time pissed off at him for just showing up like that. It was cold out, and I wasn't in the mood to chat.

"Whatever," I said, hurrying past him into the street.

"Bye-bye Birdie," Rad called out.

Chapter

4

ON SATURDAY MORNING I WOKE UP DRY-MOUTHED, WITH A thick headache that felt more like a dullness than pain. The real pain didn't begin until I went downstairs and had to sit across the table from my mother. As I tried to swallow bites of cereal, her high-pitched, locked-jaw voice made my teeth hurt.

"Such a pleasure to see you this morning," she said as she arranged dried flowers in a vase. "Oh, I'm sorry, did I say morning? Silly of me—morning is when you came home, isn't it? Now it's almost one in the afternoon. How funny! It was the cereal that fooled me."

I sipped at my orange juice and stared at a withered leaf that had dropped on the tabletop.

"Were you drinking last night?" she continued, not even looking at me, just pushing strands of dyed hair back behind her ears.

"No," I said.

It was true. I didn't drink last night. I danced until two, high on Ecstasy, and then went to the beach with Danny and some of his friends to hang out in the parking lot of the Oak Beach Inn until we got kicked out. I got home by three, but still speeding from the Ecstasy, I stayed up watching a video of Audrey Hepburn in *Love in the Afternoon* until almost five.

As my mother stood up with the flowers, she said, "Call your cousin. She's called three times this morning, looking for you. Are you supposed to go surfing today? What's that friend of hers named? Brad? He's a nice boy, will he be there? You're not bringing that Danny, are you?"

These were not questions to be answered. She was already in the next room before she finished asking them. Something in my mother's nature simply didn't allow for silence. Except for hating Danny, she didn't actually bother much with my life. I mean, if I *had* been out drinking all night, she wouldn't have minded, really. She would probably ground me for a week, but by next weekend she'd forget. With activities to plan for the tennis committee, the PTA, the Regal Community Service Group, and so on, Mom didn't have much spare energy for planning punishments. Especially not with Dad's social calendar to manage as well. Life can be overwhelming when your husband's the district attorney.

As I was slurping milk from the bottom of my bowl, my mother reappeared in the doorway. "Don't be piggish," she said.

I put down the bowl, blushing.

"I picked up some stuff for you at Bloomingdale's," she said, laying a turquoise T-shirt and a pair of cotton drawstring shorts on the back of a chair. "Maybe you can wear these when you go out today. You're not going to wear one

16

of those creepy black outfits to the beach, are you? Please do something nice with your hair. It's too pretty to always be piled up on top of your head in that insane style that you . . ."

I couldn't hear anymore because she was already heading up the stairs and down the hall to the back of the house. Fingering the clothes she'd gotten me, I laughed. What was she thinking? Had she ever *been* to the beach in October? Probably not. The sun, any time of year, could fade her naturally-red-once-it-leaves-the-bottle hair.

I put my head into my hands and rubbed the temples, hoping that the nutrition and fluids would soon start to work and the post-Ecstasy fuzz would clear. God, why did I tell Jen I would go surfing today? It wasn't even really my sport anymore. I mean, as much as my mother and I were different, at least we agreed on the evils of the sun. I lived in fear of getting, God forbid, a *tan*, which would ruin my creamy Audrey complexion. Not to mention the sun would give me a big fucking headache after I dropped E and partied all night.

Groaning, I put my dishes in the sink and headed out to the back porch. If I was going to spend the rest of the day at the beach, I'd better start getting used to the bright light of the real world now.

Squinting, I sank onto a wrought iron bench and kicked at one of the chickens my mother insisted on keeping in the yard. She said they made her feel like she had a country home. The bird squawked and took off with awkward little flying steps. Then sudden quiet footsteps made me open my eyes wide.

"Rad!" I said. "Aren't you cold?"

He was wearing a P.I.L. concert shirt that had to be at least fifteen years old. Anyway, I didn't think they made those baseball-style shirts anymore. Rad's hands looked pink and chapped, and the breeze puffed the fabric of his shirt up around him like a wave around a dock piling. I could almost see his ribs.

"You sound like music," I said, listening to his shirt flapping, his corduroys brushing, his neatly-placed footsteps and the eerie humming of his guitar strings. The body of the guitar beat like a bass drum against his hip as he walked.

Smiling, Rad sat next to me on the bench. For a second I was nervous. God, what would my mother say if she saw *him* out here? The thought of her shrieks made me cringe. Then, just for a second, I had to wonder how Rad knew where I lived. But in his presence it didn't seem important. It felt predestined. Or like a mystery I had already read but couldn't remember whodunit. It didn't really matter. My hangover was enough for me to concentrate on for the moment. Reasoning and all that would have to come later, when my sight and hearing were back to normal and my stomach wasn't churning.

"Hey, I'm sorry I was bitchy yesterday afternoon," I said, stuffing my hands deep into the pockets of my robe. "You scared me, showing up out of nowhere like that."

Rad patted my knee, and I got a sudden, warm kind of chill. *"Don't worry honey, and don't look back / The past is past, let it fade to black,"* he said.

"I'm sorry anyway," I said, not really listening too closely. I was more interested in the way his goatee

18

seemed to fade in and out of existence, depending on how the sun hit it. Weird, I thought. Cool, but weird.

"How do you do that?" I asked. "Just show up like that, or like this, out of nowhere?"

"It's you girl, and you should know it," he said, as his whole face flickered.

Whoa, I thought, this is one major hangover. "No, wait," I said. "Quit with the song shit. I mean it. Where are you coming from? Why do I even know you? You're not friends with anyone I know . . ."

"What if I'm a mermaid," he said, laughing at me, teasing.

"That's not funny," I said. "Could you please be a real person for just one minute? *Are* you real?"

Rad rolled his eyes and shook his head. Getting up, he shuffled away from me.

"You're creeping me out," I said.

As he went down the steps, making his own music again, he said, *"Sometimes I give myself the creeps."*

And he was gone. I ran to the edge of the porch to ask him to come back, but all I saw in the curve of the driveway were a couple of chickens pecking at the gravel.

Shaking my head, which had stopped hurting, I went back inside to call Jen.

I'd known Jen since I was a baby, and she was still the most normal person I knew. Maybe the *only* normal person I knew. You couldn't find anything out of the ordinary about Jen, no matter how hard you tried. And believe me, I had. After a while I'd given up and just let her be my reality anchor.

Between Jen keeping me grounded, and now Rad mysteriously appearing all the time, I felt less scared of myself. They balanced me. I felt less like I might go careening off into chaos. It was more like I was on a path, going somewhere. I just needed to know *where*.

Chapter

5

JEN PICKED ME UP IN HER '95 RED MUSTANG CONVERTIBLE. Like Jen, it was just fabulous enough to be very cool but not pretentious, which a brand-new car might have been. Not that Jen couldn't afford a new car every year if she wanted, but driving a slightly used vehicle made her fit in just about anywhere. Between her smile and her car she couldn't lose—except maybe by hanging out with me.

The car was crowded with Jen's friends, including the guy from the country club, Brad. He sat in the back, smoking a joint. As we got onto the causeway to the beach, he offered it to me.

"Brad!" Jen said, glaring at him. "Not in my car! Jesus Christ, how many times—"

"*Fine,*" he said, wetting the tips of his fingers to put the joint out.

I wouldn't have smoked anyway, not with Jen around.

"How's the new house?" I asked.

"You have to come over," Jen said. "My room is *incredible*! And I told you we have a stable and ring, so I can ride

Lucky whenever I want now. I think he misses you. You haven't seen him in like a year."

"Maybe after the beach," I said, though I didn't really care about her horse. Personally, I thought Lucky smelled. Although I liked doing a lot of the things Jen did, so far I'd never let her convince me to try riding.

"It's so great that we live nearby now," she said. "I just wish we had the same lunch period, so we could hang out more at school."

"I usually sit with Danny, anyway. You'd be bored."

Brad groaned from the backseat. I knew he was rolling his eyes, but I didn't turn around, like he wanted me to.

"Shut up, Brad," said Rachel, who *was* in my lunch period and always tried to sit at Danny's table. "I think Danny's cute. Don't listen to him, Cary. You're really lucky to be going out with a babe like that."

I just shrugged. Of course I was lucky.

• • •

When we got to Field Three at Robert Moses Beach, we went straight to the snack counter. Jen knew the manager from last summer, when she had tried slumming and had worked there for a month. Using her special smile, she got us all scrambled egg sandwiches, *free*, even though breakfast was long over. I took one, squirted on twice as much ketchup as there was egg, and ate next to Jen on the sandy metal picnic bench.

"I mean, bodyboarding is fun," she said between bites, "but I don't see why you don't keep practicing your real surfing. I keep telling you, once you get the hang of it, it's way better."

"I like being closer to the water," I said, finishing my

sandwich and rubbing number twenty sunscreen on my face in thick strokes.

"What, does bouncing around on the board give you an orgasm or something?" Brad said.

"Grow up," Jen said.

"*Really*," Rachel added as we left the snickering guys to put on our wet suits in the dressing room.

• • •

"Come on, what's he like? Is he big?" Rachel asked me in the dressing room.

She was in the open stall across from me, and Jen was hopping around in the aisle, trying to pull up her suit. Turning around, I blushed. Not that I was attracted to either of them, but seeing them naked made me feel funny, like I was invading their privacy or something. I was afraid if my eyes accidentally looked at a nipple or something, they'd know something about me and think I was checking them out, maybe even trying to come on to them.

I hated putting on my wet suit. It was so tiring. I always felt like by the time I pulled the damn thing on, I wouldn't have any strength left to swim. Trying to squeeze my hand through the sleeve, I banged my elbow on the side of the stall, hitting the funny bone.

"Come *on*, we know you've *obviously* been fucking him. You've been going out *forever*," Rachel said. "But you never give us any dirt."

I tried to focus on the pain in my elbow so I wouldn't get embarrassed. I hated these female bonding things, where you had to give up every detail of your sex life. It was supposed to be *guys* who did this in the locker room, but I swear I think girls are the worst. I can't look at anyone Jen or Rachel dates because I already know the length, width and circumference of his dick, how long he takes to come and what his favorite position is. Sometimes I just start giggling. It's like I not only have sex with Danny, I have to have sex with practically every guy I know through these locker room discussions.

And it doesn't interest me that much.

But as I zipped Jen's wet suit for her, I gave in and told them how Danny's hair smells and feels. I told them that Danny's penis is flat and squarish. That was enough, and then Rachel started laughing about what Brad was like in bed, which I really didn't want to know about. But at least it got me off the hook.

"Damn, your new suit looks rad," Jen said, changing the subject as we left the dressing room.

"Yeah, I love the lavender stripes," said Rachel.

"Thanks, I got it at Southwick Surf when I bought the new board."

The guys were waiting for us outside, and they rolled their eyes as we continued to talk about clothes and stuff. For a second I wanted to say, shut up before I tell everyone how *you* can't come unless you're on top, and *you* had sex with your best friend's cousin, and *you* . . . but I'd never do that. I did wonder, though, if while we were talking about sex in the dressing room, they were secretly discussing fashion.

● ● ●

It was getting late by the time we hit the water, and the ocean was actually warmer than the windy air. It would be for a couple more weeks, then the water would catch up to the season and I'd have to start wearing the feet of my wet suit. Wading in with my boogie board under my arm, I felt the salt water seep into my suit, making my skin clammy for a few seconds before the suit sucked itself tight around me. I felt like I was wearing a giant condom.

The tide was just changing, making the incoming waves a little rough, but good for surfing. Still, even at its roughest, the ocean here was gentle compared to most other beaches because of the barrier reef. You could feel safe here and concentrate on catching a good wave without worrying about a bad current dragging you under and out.

That didn't make it less exhausting to swim out. The little waves in front sent froth spinning up my nose as I pushed over them to the bigger swells farther out. Jen and the others were already lying on their boards facing the shore, waiting to ride in, while I was still fighting the surf. Because I was a weak swimmer, I missed the first good wave coming in and ended up getting pummeled and tossed as it broke on top of me. Sputtering, I fought my way back onto my board and turned to wait again.

Catching a wave is as scary as it is thrilling. You have to wait until it starts to curl right over you—that same moment, as a kid, I always knew to dive *under* it before it crashed. But instead of going under now, I waited as it started to break, then turned away from it and windmilled my arms as hard and fast as I could to pull on top of the foam. When I caught it, it was like flying. I flattened my arms against my sides and let the sea sweep me to shore, on top of the water, barely touching it. It took me all the way in, until my board was flat on the sand and the water drew back, sucking at my ankles. For a minute I lay there on my belly, the water flowing in and out until I was sunk into the wet sand like a relief sculpture. Then heading back out again, with the ocean swirling around my legs, then beating against my belly, and finally splashing up my nose, I forgot who I was. I became part of the water and the tide.

"Come on, Cary," Jen shouted, "Don't space out now! We only have time to catch a few more before it gets dark!"

She should've sounded annoyed, since it was *my* hangover that had made us leave so late for the beach. But since she was Jen, she just sounded normal.

In the ocean, with my hair pulled back in a simple ponytail like Jen's and my new wet suit on, I felt as normal as her. Paddling with my hands and feet, I raced her back in to the bigger waves. We caught one at the same time, and as I skittered towards shore, I could see her gracefully balancing on her board, curving over the surf, all focus and inner calm. Suddenly I thought, maybe I *will* go see Lucky tonight. Maybe I'm missing out, not learning to ride. Life can't be all sex and drugs, clubs and Danny, and pieces of Wendy's sweaters.

• • •

I was the last one out of the dressing room. The sun was going down, and I was shivering and crinkled from the cold shower I had taken. But I was smiling as I headed to the parking lot, where Jen was playfully honking her horn at me. I started to jog.

Rad was sitting in the back of a pickup, one of the green ones the people who worked at the beach used. I passed him on my way to Jen's car and waved.

26

"I can't talk now," I said. "My cousin's waiting. I'm going to see her horse."

"*Shiny happy people*," he said, and I grinned because right then that was exactly how I felt. Jen honked again, and I ran faster.

Chapter

6

My mother was in the living room when I got home from Danny's the next Friday. She wore a Chanel pantsuit, and around her neck was a slender gold chain with a small but expensive emerald drop. As she flitted around the room, organizing hors d'oeuvres and waiters, her sprayed hair never moved. I was amazed at how the elegant sculpture of red balanced so neatly on top of her head.

"Your father will be home in an hour, so please make yourself presentable. We're having guests," she said as she blew past me.

"I noticed. But I'm going out tonight."

My mother rolled her eyes. Then she sighed. "Just as well," she said. "Oh, and your eyeliner is smeared."

Wiping at my eyes, I headed upstairs to my room. Pulling an airbrushed painting of a unicorn off the wall behind my bed, I carefully removed the cardboard I'd taped behind it. On the cardboard, under a thin sheet of tissue paper, was my Wendy collection. From my purse I pulled this week's contraband—some paint I had peeled from her bedpost. On it you could see half a faded flower that had been painted on it. Very carefully, so it wouldn't crumble, I taped it to the cardboard next to last week's sweater fluff. For a minute I stared at my collection and pictured Wendy in my mind. Then, before it could make me sad, I put the cardboard back against the picture frame and rehung the painting.

Back in the kitchen I snatched a plate of fancy hors d'oeuvres and took them to my room with a glass of champagne. There were little slices of smoked salmon with cucumber slivers and dill sprigs on toast triangles; anchovy paste and French cheese on crackers; hard-boiled-egg slices and caviar, and little puffs of something rich and sticky. I ate it all by the light of a big, red Jesus candle I'd found at the Good Samaritan thrift shop.

My hair was too much of a mess to fix, so I had to start from scratch, carefully pinning each wisp into place. Soon, I decided, I'm going to cut it off. I'll get one of those sassy Audrey cuts, like in *Roman Holiday*. I'll go to Jen's hairdresser, not my mother's.

From my closet I chose a taffeta dress with a full skirt and a cinched waist. The neckline was a wide "V" that extended to the edges of my shoulders, showing off my long neck and sharp collarbones. Taking off the pearls I wore at school, I switched to a necklace of blood red, multifaceted plastic stones and matching teardrop earrings. When I'd painted my nails the same red and glued on my false eyelashes, I sipped at the glass of champagne. Downstairs, I knew my father had arrived with some of the early guests. His big reelect-me laugh filled the house. I knew my mother would be on the sofa with some of the ladies, smiling until it hurt but somehow enjoying herself anyway. Later my father would draw her into a discussion with the boys about local politics, proving that he was a man of the nineties. My mother, who reads six newspapers a day, including one in Spanish and one in Japanese, would make a great impression. Before I got back home, everyone would be happily tipsy and on their way home. And in the morning they'd all remember how delightful the hors d'oeuvres were.

I knew I'd have to slip out the back door to meet Danny at the curb. Not that I couldn't parade through the party, but I'm not that mean. Since my parents are good enough to stay out of my life most of the time, I try to spare them the trouble of having to explain me to their friends.

• • •

At eight, Danny picked me up in his father's truck. He was playing the stereo loudly, and smoking cigarettes out the window because he knew the smell bothered me. For some reason, he didn't get it that the wind whipping through the small cab of the truck and blowing my hair into my eyes bothered me more than a little smoke. I fumbled in the ashtray for a joint and lit it, inhaling until my eyes watered.

• • •

In Phantasie's parking lot, Danny passed out hits of Ecstasy and collected money. Then we went inside. I got a big glass of water at the bar right away so I could avoid the dehydration I'd get from the Ecstasy. Already Danny was at the head of a table in the corner, saving a seat for me and watching as his lame friends tried to make eye contact with a group of girls. A half hour later, high, we started dancing.

The music didn't matter; I could hardly hear it. All that mattered was the beat, deep and throbbing up from the floor. With Ecstasy, the beat and my body were parts of a whole, inseparable. I danced without conscience or doubt, and Danny's touch felt like sparks. On drugs it was so easy to be in love, and to dance. I even danced with a couple of Danny's friends so they wouldn't feel like total losers, dancing by themselves.

After a couple hours I went back to our table to gulp down more water. My hands tapped the beat on the table-top, and my eyes flitted around the room, observing without really focusing. Suddenly a group of girls near the bathroom caught my eye. I'd seen them around school. Behind their backs everyone called them "the Lesbian Collective."

"Check out the dykes," said Brian to Danny as they joined me at the table.

He was pointing at the girls by the bathroom, and as Danny grinned I cringed, hiding my face behind my glass. Danny put his arm around me and some water spilled down the front of my dress. I shivered.

"Why don't you go talk to them, Bri?" said John, the pimply boy. "You probably have a better chance of getting laid by a dyke than a straight bitch."

"Don't say bitch," Danny said, noticing when I stiffened.

Rolling their eyes, Brian and John hopped back to the dance floor with the beat. Meanwhile, out of the corner of my eye I watched the lesbian girls hanging out by the bathroom. A couple of the girls were too heavy for me. One had beautiful hair and a mysterious parched face, but her legs were too spindly-long, and I didn't like the way she dressed. One was attractive in a traditional kind of way, but she reminded me too much of Jen, and that gave me chills. Only one of the girls seemed even remotely my type, and she was hanging onto one of the big girls, obviously unavailable. Not that I was searching for someone anyway.

Still watching them, I cuddled closer to Danny and kissed his knuckles when his hand brushed my face. I wouldn't want to be in a clique like that. I mean, in school those girls were never separated. It was like they couldn't stand on their own. I guessed it must be hard, but I still didn't like the almost political force they tried to be, and meanwhile people still laughed at them from across the room. Besides being pathetic, it pissed me off that their public hand-holding and kissing had nothing to do with love. It was more like they were spitting in unison at the rest of us.

I was just thinking how nice it was to be with Danny, who wasn't trying to impress anyone by holding *my* hand, when I saw Wendy weaving out of the bathroom. My fingers stopped tapping for a second and I gulped, overwhelmed by how gorgeous she was next to all the other girls. As she stopped to talk to the gay girls, my heart warmed and beat faster. I wondered if maybe all Wendy's skeevy boyfriends were just a cover, and really—

Before I could finish my thought, Danny had jumped up, rocking the table and almost knocking over my glass. I stared at him in shock.

"What the fuck is she doing?" he said, watching Wendy teeter and lean into the parched-faced girl. There was lots of giggling by the bathroom as the girls propped Wendy up against the wall.

Danny pushed his way through the crowd to his sister, and I followed. "Excuse me," he said to the girls with strained politeness, "that's my sister. I'll take care of her."

"She's cute," teased one of the big girls as Danny shoved his arm under Wendy and started leading her away.

"She has a *boy*friend," he said.

"Nice guy you got there," said the Jen type, darkly. Her friend elbowed her and giggled. I blushed.

As Danny headed for the door, I told the girl, "He's just upset. It's been a long night. He *is* a nice guy."

The girl shrugged. "Whatever. His sister is real cute, though. I love the purple lining on her eyebrows. Very dangerous."

The girl seemed to wink at me then, and it gave me the creeps, big-time. It made me mad too. What gave her the right to act like we thought alike? What made her think I wanted to share inside jokes with her and her snotty friends?

"Cary!" Danny yelled from the doorway. "Come on!"

Weaving frantically through the dancing bodies, I finally made it outside and followed Danny to his pickup. He propped Wendy up between us, and she giggled for a few seconds before passing out. I wished I could pass out myself, but it had only been a few hours since I had dropped the E and I was speeding so fast I was sweating.

Luckily, my parents were sleeping when I got home.

33

The carpet was thick in their room, so it was easy to tiptoe through to their bathroom and sneak a couple of my mother's sleeping pills.

In my room, waiting for the pill to work, I let my hair down and changed into a flannel nightgown. Sitting on my old rocking horse, I frantically pet its ropy mane, willing my hands to stop shaking and my scalp to stop tingling. I picked up the phone and dialed a random number. It worked, as I knew it would.

"Rad? I'm glad you're up. Can you talk?"

"There are many things I would like to say to you," he sang.

"Do you think I'm crazy? What's wrong with me?" I asked.

"I just figure everything is cool," he said.

"But do you think those girls know about me? What if they start telling everyone in school?"

Rad sighed and strummed his guitar, which sounded weird over the phone line. *"Don't let them break up your mind,"* he said.

"Maybe I'm full of shit and I don't even know it," I said, twisting the phone cord around my finger. The sleeping pill was starting to work, and I felt calmer. "Maybe I don't even love Wendy. I just admire her. You know— want to be like her or something."

"She says love is not what she's after / But everybody knows," Rad said.

I rocked harder on my painted horse, not caring if the creaking woke up my parents. *"Everybody* knows? How could anyone know what *I'm* not even sure about? I could've been imagining that girl's stupid wink. I bet those girls don't know *anything!"*

34

"The roots of our imaginations can't go on indefinitely," Rad said, and then all I heard was the dial tone.

I wanted to call him back right away and ask him what he meant, but I couldn't remember the number. And deep down, I knew what he meant. He meant I should open my eyes and see people as they *are*. Wendy and Danny were *real* people, not just symbols of my confused lust and lack of direction. Rad was refusing to tell me what to do. I guess being my guardian angel was a part-time position.

Still, rather than give up my fantasy world, I tried to dial Rad's number again, by just letting my fingers dance over the buttons, but the numbers wouldn't come. My hand was sluggish now, and I felt sleepy. The whole phone conversation was sliding into memory, and I didn't care anymore as I climbed under my comforter. I put my thumb in my mouth and sucked it as I slipped into sleep.

Chapter

7

My mother prided herself on being active in the community, but even if she weren't, she probably would've gone to that Monday's school board meeting. Everybody was going. They were having an open discussion of the high school's curriculum. Even though Babylon was still mostly white middle class, every year it got a little more diverse. I could remember when I was in sixth grade, there was one black boy in my grade. Now there were four black kids in my AP English class and two Puerto Ricans and a new Asian girl in my homeroom. There was talk of expanding the curriculum to include history about and literature by people of all races, creeds and so on.

Even the students were going to the meeting. We were mostly in favor of the "Rainbow Curriculum," and we were nervous. No one knew how their parents might embarrass them in front of the entire school. I was especially nervous because Danny and Wendy's parents would be there. I'd never met them before. I wasn't sure if Danny was embarrassed by them, or by me. But ever since we'd been going out, he'd deftly managed to keep us from cross-ing paths.

• • •

Jen and her parents came to my house before the meeting. My aunt looked me up and down, evaluating my cigarette pants and thrift shop sweater. Then she gave my mother a smile that said, "Kids these days."

"Don't you look lovely!" my Uncle Greg said to me. "Margaret, remember when you had a sweater like that? You know, we should check your mother's attic. I bet she's saved some of your old clothes from when you were in high school. Cary might like to pick through it all. Would you like that, Cary?"

Aunt Maggie kept smiling while I shrugged.

"Brought you something," Uncle Greg said, holding his hands behind his back.

"Dad!" Jen said, turning red.

But I didn't care. We always played this game. I picked the right hand, and Uncle Greg gave me a grape lollipop. He was a pediatrician.

"We'd better get moving," my father said as my mother straightened his tie.

• • •

The auditorium was packed, parents in front and stu-dents clustered around the back, standing room only. A few brave ones were outside on the steps, smoking ciga-rettes. Wendy was there, of course. I tried not to keep glancing back out the window at her.

"Over here," I whispered to Jen, leading her over to

where I saw Danny standing in the corner. She followed me but kept scanning the crowd, looking for Rachel or one of her other friends. Which was okay with me. I grabbed Danny's hand and squeezed it.

"Where are your parents?" I asked him.

"That's them, standing up now," he said, cringing. "I gotta go outside. They're killing me."

Danny left, and I pushed forward so I could hear better. I didn't have to. Danny's father, Mr. Waterman, was shouting.

"Now you listen," he said. The thin wisps of hair on his head went askew as he shook, screaming with his whole body. "When I moved my family here, it wasn't easy. Property taxes are sky high. The commute to my shop is a bitch. But I said to my wife, it's for the kids. We don't need to worry about guns and drugs here. Our kids can get a good education here."

Danny's mother bobbed her head like a pigeon. She was holding on tightly to her husband's meaty arm, and now she tugged at it. He bent, and she whispered in his ear. I noticed how much she looked like Wendy, full-breasted but slender, almost skinny. Age wrinkled around the sharp bones in her face, but you could still tell she had been pretty.

"I'm not saying there's anything wrong with people knowing their own cultures, or whatever," Mr. Waterman continued. "All I'm saying is we all live in America now, and what's wrong with all our kids learning about *American* history? Excuse me for saying so, but our founding fathers didn't ride the Mayflower over from Puerto Rico."

My mother stood up. "I don't think that's the issue here, sir. No one wants to eliminate or change the history our children are studying. We're only considering adding to it."

Go Mom, I thought, suddenly proud.

Mr. Waterman, who hadn't sat down when my mother started talking, continued shouting. "No offense, ma'am, but there's only so many hours in a school day. There's plenty of reading, writing and arithmetic already. Where we gonna put this extra 'culture?' Maybe your kid has time for some extra reading at home, but my boy works at a gas station twelve hours a week."

"We're not talking about that much—" my mother began.

"So what are we talking about, some token gesture?" piped up a voice from the back, the student section. It was one of the girls from Phantasie, one of the gay girls. The big one with the gritty voice, Renee.

She continued, "Like, in English we'll read *two* poems by Langston Hughes, instead of just the one we read now?"

"No, dear, we're not—" began one of the board members.

"Okay," Renee said, "and what about subcultures? How come no one's brought up gay literature and gay history?"

My mother and Danny's parents started talking all at once, along with several other parents. My father stayed in his seat, because a lot of his constituency was here. He had to wait until he saw for sure which way the crowd was going before he could express himself.

"Excuse my French, but what do dykes and queers have to do with education?" Mr. Waterman said, his big fists clenched and his face sweaty-red.

"This is a discussion, not a place for name-calling," said another parent.

Then my mother started in, her voice commanding attention even over Mr. Waterman's bellow. "Although I do not like his choice of words, I understand and sympathize with the gentleman's question."

Oh my God, I thought, shrinking back. I could hardly breathe.

"We are talking tonight about expanding our children's cultural knowledge. This is not a discussion of the sex education curriculum. Not that that isn't an important issue, but it is one to discuss at another time."

A mother stood up, and next to her, her daughter. The girl's new, I thought. Or else why would she be sitting down there with the parents? There was a boy there, too, younger, still sitting.

Putting her arm around her daughter's shoulders, the woman said, "It's only because of the deficit in our own educations that we perceive homosexuality as something only to be discussed in sex ed. classes, if it is to be discussed at all. We need to recognize this entire subculture, which exists in all races and classes . . ."

Some students clapped, some giggled. What amazed me, and kept me from running outside to avoid it all, was the girl. There she was, standing in the middle of a couple hundred parents and being stared at by practically the entire school, and she didn't even lower her head. The boy—I guessed it was her brother—had slipped farther down in his seat with every word his mother said, but the girl stood tall, mesmerizing me.

"What does your husband have to say about this?" a man from the front row shouted. "Or maybe you're a dyke?"

Someone on the board banged a gavel until the shouting died down. Of course, then it was my mother who spoke first.

"I understand the concern of some of the young people here," my mother said, smiling. "And as much as parents would like to think otherwise, we know the most important thing on our kids' minds is sex."

Several parents chuckled on cue.

My mother continued, "But that is something we as parents must each address at home."

Oh no, I thought. We're not going to have one of *those* talks tonight, are we?

"So I think if we could pause for a moment to regain our senses, we can get back to the discussion at hand."

As most of the group nodded, the new girl's mother tossed up her hands and, shaking her head, sat down. The girl remained standing and she stared straight at my mother. I was astounded by how alike they looked at that moment, totally unflinching. The drama was too much for me, and as I started pushing back toward the door, the girl said, "Don't we, the students, have any say in this?"

"Not really, dear," said my mother.

• • •

I went to bed that night with my mother's calm voice ripping through me and repeating itself in my head: "Danny's father made some interesting points. It's a shame he can't express himself with less anger. Cary, do you know anyone at Babylon who's gay?"

Chapter

TUESDAY I WAS IN FOURTH-PERIOD STUDY HALL, TRYING TO concentrate on my calculus homework. Study hall for seniors was held in the lunchroom so people could get coffee and bagels and mostly just fool around. It was assumed that by senior year your future was already determined and it no longer mattered much what you did.

As I penciled the derivative of a long equation into my notebook, the Lesbian Collective settled in at my table. I ignored them, but the smell of a toasted bagel with cream cheese made my stomach rumble. They crunched loudly on their food, but I didn't look up, even to say hello. Why did they have to sit at *my* table? Sweat trickled over the pearls around my neck. My mother had looked so relieved when I had told her last night that no, I didn't personally know anyone who was gay.

"Remember Allison from the gymnastics team last year?" one of the girls said, chewing.

"Oh God," said a gritty voice, "you mean *Barbie*?"

"I liked her floor routine," said someone else, quietly.

"I *bet* you did!" said Gritty, laughing and chewing some more.

I tried not to roll my eyes or blush. Instead, I scribbled nonsense in my notebook and kept listening.

"Okay, get this now," said the first girl, who I noticed was the parched-faced girl from Phantasie. "She went to U. Conn., and my sister said that now Allison's a proud bisexual. Can you believe that shit?"

"Oh *God*."

"What, does she belong to like one of those groups, like Rights for Gays, or some crap?"

"I don't know, but you'd better believe the whole campus knows she's got a girlfriend, like anyone cares!"

"The liberal Barbie doll with the anatomically incorrect Ken."

"Ken with a cootchie."

I almost laughed at that, but instead I turned a page in my textbook and tried harder to read.

Gritty sucked cream cheese off her fingers. "I hate LUGs," she said.

"Do you know what a LUG is?" said the girl next to me, nudging me in the shoulder.

Looking up, I shrugged, acting bored and feeling embarrassed. More than embarrassed—I felt like I was coming under attack. Too many coincidences were piling up. First, the scene at Phantasie and the wink I thought I saw. Now the Collective gathers at my table, and they're talking to me. I felt like I was being tested, or auditioning for a part in their group. I didn't *want* to be one of them! Even if I was definitely gay, it wouldn't be so I could hang around with a snotty clique. It would be for Wendy.

"Maybe Allison always was gay. You just didn't know about it," I said quietly. Maybe, I thought, she didn't come out in high school *because* of you. Not everyone wants to be a stereotype. Certainly not everyone wants the whole school staring at them and making fun.

Gritty snorted, and the redheaded girl who I thought was pretty said, "LUG is Lesbian Until Graduation. It's very popular on college campuses."

Nodding once, I looked back down at my notebook. What do they care what I think anyway? I have a *boyfriend* for godsakes! That makes me a nonperson to them.

"C'mon," someone said, "who the fuck do they think they are?" She got up on the bench and teetered on Barbie toes. "Oh, look at me," she said in a shrill-sweet voice. "I have a *girlfriend*, and I'm so *cool*! Everybody loves me, even *gay* people. I'm majoring in Women's Studies, and I'm discovering who I really am. Everybody look at me!"

Everyone laughed, and I started fumbling in my purse for change, thinking now would be a good time to get up for a cup of coffee.

The quiet girl spoke up. "What if she really is gay? How do you know she hasn't finally found her soul mate?"

"Oh, *please*," said parched-face. "I just feel sorry for her girlfriend. I hope *she* knows she's only an experiment."

"Really. I mean, how many nice girls do you think are going to be hurt before sweet Allison finds herself a hubby and settles down in the suburbs with kids and a dog?"

"Hey, I *like* dogs!"

"Oh, shut up, you!" said the red-haired girl, and everyone giggled.

They stopped talking and resumed eating their bagels, so I stopped looking for change and started on the next calculus problem. Realizing I'd been holding my breath, I softly exhaled and sucked in fresh air deeply but quietly, trying to be invisible.

Suddenly one of the big girls leaned close to me. I could smell her onion breath. "Can you imagine what it's like, finding out your girlfriend, the one you're afraid to tell your parents about, is *bi*? Which means she leaves you for a *guy*, like you meant nothing to her?"

"Yeah," chimed in Gritty. "It'd be like if your sexy boyfriend suddenly told you he was leaving you and running off with . . . *that* guy!"

I looked where she was pointing, and when I saw it was at Danny's friend, pimply-John, I had to laugh. The other girls started giggling, too, and I no longer felt so uncomfortable. In fact, I felt a little stupid and paranoid. I'd been so sure they were attacking me. But now I saw they were just making conversation about something they knew. What were they supposed to talk about, my calculus homework?

I felt bad about judging them. Yeah, they could be snotty, but what choice did they have? Being gay wasn't easy at Babylon High. They *had* to stand together. They took the crap—all the bad jokes and backward glances—for everyone in school who ever even thought about falling in love with someone of the same sex.

"Hey, Cary, what's up?"

It was Jen. She slid onto the corner of the bench next to me.

"Jen!" I said, "Do you know . . ."

46

The girls introduced themselves in staccato tones. "Paula." "Deena." "Natasha." "Renee." "Lisa."

"Hi, I'm Jen," Jen said, bright as usual, holding out her hand to shake.

Only quiet-Lisa reached out and limply accepted Jen's hand. I didn't get it. Everyone likes Jen. I was aware of an eerie, frozen silence as Jen chattered at me. Although I was glad Jen wasn't physically dragging me away, like Danny had "rescued" Wendy on Friday night, I wished she'd go away. Or maybe that they would go away. Anything, so long as I wouldn't be stuck sitting here in this weird situation. Jen wasn't stupid. If the Lesbian Collective kept glaring at her, she'd remember that they had been laughing a second ago, and that I had been laughing with them. What kind of signals would that give her? It was wrong, it was wimpy, but I cared what Jen thought of me. A lot.

"So," she said, "I'm totally glad I saw you here. Do you want to go surfing again this weekend? I'm trying to figure out how many people I'll have to squeeze into my car."

"Paula, you want to go outside and smoke?" said parched-Natasha.

They got up, and Jen smiled at them. When they smiled back, they looked excessively friendly. Paula took red-headed-Deena's hand and led her away from the table, too, kissing her cheek loudly enough that people from other tables turned to look.

Not noticing, or not caring, Jen continued, "I don't know why you don't bring Danny along. I have an extra board . . ."

Renee announced in her gritty voice, "I'm going to the bathroom. Lisa, do you have that lipstick I like?"

Nodding, Lisa followed Renee toward the bathroom, clutching her purse with twig-like fingers. They left the table cluttered with napkins, Styrofoam cups and half-eaten food.

"Would any of your friends like to go with us Saturday?" Jen asked, gesturing at the now deserted table. "God, I'm so rude! I'm really sorry, Cary. I should've asked them right away. No wonder they looked mad."

"They're not my friends," I said, closing my calculus book. "They were just sitting here."

"Oh," Jen said. "Anyway, think about Saturday, and let me know soon so I can reserve a place for you in the car. Listen, I've got to go. I have to get the English notes from Rachel before the test. See you later?"

I nodded and stared at the empty bench after she left.

"Can you see them, see right through them?" said Rad, filling the empty space. *"That same old crowd / Was like a cold, dark cloud."*

"What makes me mad," I said, not at all surprised to see Rad, "is that I was almost starting to like them. Or at least understand them a little. Until they treated Jen like that. I practically could've respected them."

Rad rubbed his fingers along the strings of his guitar, making them hum. The knot in his bandanna bobbed up and down when he swallowed. I knew he understood what I meant when he said, *"The way they talk about each other / The way they talk about themselves . . ."*

"Exactly," I said, staring at the bandanna, hypnotized. "It's like they have a purpose, and they don't have to wonder or worry. They know where they're going, and even where they are."

When Rad laughed, it sounded like the little wind chimes in my mother's sunroom. He smiled with wide, thin lips of perfect pink as he said, *"And all the roads that lead you there are winding / And all the lights that light the way are blinding."*

Yeah, I thought, exactly. I didn't want to be stereotyped. But I could definitely see the comfort and strength in being exactly what was expected of you.

As the bell rang, I saw the Lesbian Collective across the cafeteria, all together again and moving in the same direction.

Chapter

9

"CAN YOU ROLL FOR ME?" WENDY ASKED. "MY HANDS ARE full."

We were on our way to Phantasie, and she was wedged between me and Danny in his truck. She handed me paper and a little bag of pot. Her scent wrapped around me like a snake, almost choking me with pleasure. She and Danny smelled similar on the surface, like the same shampoo, laundry detergent and dinner, with a hint of vodka and weed. But Wendy's smell was deep, with a fuzzy sweetness that made me want to suck it in and hold it in my lungs, not breathing anymore.

While she fiddled with a brush, teasing her hair, I leaned closer and rolled a joint for her. I must've been pretty high already, because for a second I thought she rubbed her knee against mine, on purpose. I started to inch my foot next to hers, when her knee moved away again, and I realized it was just that Danny had been shifting gears and had bumped into her. Still, that spot on my knee was left hot and tingling.

I wished I'd sat in the middle so I could cling to Danny

while we drove, but instead I finished rolling the joint and leaned my head against the cool, misty window. Trying to concentrate on the door handle stabbing into my side, I watched Wendy's legs shiver with the truck's movement, lean in olive stockings and silvery-pink shoes. My head started to feel like it was collapsing in on me, so I stopped staring at Wendy and looked instead at Danny's hands, rich with veins and lines.

In the club's parking lot, after I did my hit of E, I began to feel itchy with annoyance at Danny as he made his drug deals. It was really starting to bug me, being practically invisible whenever Danny had something else to do. God! Sometimes he was just like my father, running everything based on his schedule and his needs and assuming that the world would accommodate him. Someday, I thought. Then, yeah right, Cary, someday what?

"I can't believe Keith isn't fucking here yet," Danny said, clutching the last hit of Ecstasy in his fist. "He *knows* I'm not going to stand out here all night. If he's not here in five minutes . . ."

Wendy was starting to ease away, swinging her hips toward the door. I said quickly, "I'm cold. I'm going inside. I'll meet you there."

Danny almost looked surprised, and I almost smiled, then he put his hand behind my head, pulled me close and kissed me.

"Right on," he said. "I'll catch you in a few."

As I turned to follow Wendy, Danny brushed his hand over my ass, lifting my dress a little. He kissed my neck just barely, and for a second he smelled exactly like Wendy. I had to force myself to move.

51

• • •

Inside, I went directly to Danny's corner table to wait for him and for the E to kick in, to separate me from the crowd yet still make me a part of the whole scene. It felt comforting to be like one limb on a pulsing creature, no longer alone with my own thoughts.

"That's a hip dress," Wendy said, already at the table and leaning back in her chair. She blew smoke rings easily.

Blushing, I said, "Thanks, I got it in the city over the summer at Cheap Jack's by Union—"

"Uh-huh," Wendy said. "So, do you know some cool places to hang out in the city? You know, clubs and stuff? This place is getting dull."

I was starting to shake. This was the longest Wendy had ever paid attention to me, and I didn't want to blow it. I was glad she'd noticed my dress, which fit tightly around my waist and hips, with a high slit up the leg.

"I guess," I said, even though I didn't know anything. I mostly only went out to places Danny took me to. Which was basically his bedroom, under the bleachers at school and here.

"Like where? Maybe sometime you could take me around," Wendy said.

"What's taking Danny so long?" I said, looking around frantically.

"I know some people think you're weird, the way you dress, but at least you have a style," Wendy said.

I twisted my hands in my lap, digging my right thumbnail into the palm of my left hand to keep calm. Practically whispering, I said, "I never thought you noticed . . ."

Continuing as though she hadn't heard me, Wendy said, "Not like the other rich bitches, with their neatly torn Gap jeans and two-hundred-dollar sneakers. God, like that girl, Jen. You know her, don't you?"

Wendy's eyes sparkled as she leaned close to me, like we were sharing a secret. It was becoming hard to breathe.

"She's my cousin," I said. "She's cool when you get to know her. Everybody likes—"

Before I could defend Jen anymore, Wendy bounced up to her feet and grabbed my hand. I couldn't tell if she was fucking with my head, or if we'd made a connection, but I was afraid to wonder too much.

"Let's dance," she said.

I followed her to the dance floor, the drugs ringing in my ears. People cleared space for Wendy, and we danced in front of each other, not touching, but electrically charged, it seemed to me. As I sank into the beat of the music, Wendy didn't seem so scary or unapproachable. I felt like I could reach out and touch her if I wanted, and all that kept me from doing it was that I was afraid the current would stop my heart.

Suddenly Wendy leaned close. For a second, I flushed. I thought she was going to kiss me on the neck, like Danny always did.

Instead she whispered, "Fucking gorgeous guy. Gotta go."

And she was gone, sashaying in her special way and rolling her shoulders as she approached a skinny guy with a perfectly shaved head and a dragon tattoo etched into his skull over his ear. I'd seen Wendy hanging around him before. I didn't want to crumple in front of everyone, so I tried to make it to the bathroom. I passed Danny on the way and brushed against him, but I barely felt his kiss. I was folding in on myself. How could I have been so stupid? For a second I thought Wendy might actually like me. Even love me. Ha ha.

I ran into the bathroom and locked myself in a toilet stall.

"What're you doing in there, having children?" someone yelled, banging on the stall door.

Obviously, I couldn't hide on the toilet seat all night, so I moved out of the stall to a corner next to the sinks. Pretending to fix my eyelashes, I listened to the other girls talking in clipped part-sentences between thumps of the music.

"They were making out in the back of my car. Is that rude or what?"

"Do you think she's *really* a virgin?"

"I can't believe he won't even . . ."

"This techno shit is . . ."

"Your skirt's crooked . . ."

"Come on, 'Tasha, I want to dance!"

"Where's the little flake tonight anyway?"

"Did you see that guy with the dragon on his head?"

"She's such a tease."

"Hey, I'm talking to you. I said she's a tease."

Looking in the mirror, I saw Lisa, the quiet dyke, next to me.

"Sorry," I said. "What?"

"Wendy," she said. "She's a tease. Why are you always following her around?"

"She's jerking you around," said Renee in a grittierthan-usual voice from behind me. "Quit hogging the mirror."

I moved aside, shrinking deeper into the corner.

When I didn't respond to their stares, Renee rolled her eyes, and she and Lisa left. I was shaking, wondering how they could know. I suddenly wished I hadn't dropped E, because I didn't feel right. Tugging on my skirt as though it could hide me, I stepped backward into a stall, breathing in short gasps.

"Oh, sorry," I said, bumping into someone who was already in there.

Two hands cupped my face, and suddenly a tongue was deep in my mouth, and I smelled flowers and hair spray. At first I was stiff with surprise, but gradually, as the kiss continued, I relaxed and leaned closer. Then it stopped. I looked into the green eyes of Deena, the red-haired girl, who was smiling at me.

"What do you think? Everyone says I'm a great kisser," she said.

I felt stupid, standing there with my mouth still open. I choked out, "Isn't Paula your girlfriend?" How lame!

"It's only a kiss," Deena said. "Don't you ever have any fun?"

"I have a boyfriend."

"Yeah, but you were curious, weren't you?"

When I didn't answer right away, she looked hurt, but I still didn't know what to say. I just wanted to go home.

"Okay, I don't have Wendy's tits, but I'm not totally undesirable," Deena whined.

"I'm sorry," I said, wiping at my lips. I only . . . fuck, I only wanted to go home.

"Excuse me," I said, pushing out of the bathroom.

Danny was at his table, and I kissed him on the mouth desperately, trying to clear my head. He pulled me onto his lap, but when I felt the beginning of his hard-on, I stood up quickly, freaking out all over. Wendy was making out with the shaved-head guy, and I wanted to punch someone.

"I'm going out to the truck for a while," I told Danny.

"Are you okay? You want—"

"I just want to be alone. I'll be back soon."

"What happened? Is it the E?"

Danny looked too concerned for me to deal with lying, so I just shook my head hard and gently pushed him away before hurrying out to the parking lot with his keys.

In the cab of the truck I pressed my head against the steering wheel. My head, feet and hands tingled uncomfortably, like my skin was trying to crawl off. In my chest my heart beat fast. I couldn't tell if it was the drugs, or if I was going crazy. Rubbing circles on my stomach to keep my hands busy and belly settled, I pursed my lips and concentrated on exhaling the scary thoughts.

Someone tapped on the window. For a second I thought it was Danny, or worse, Wendy, and I looked up angrily.

"Oh. It's you," I said.

Using one hand to steady the other, I rolled down the window. Rad's face was chapped from the night wind. When he put a cold hand against my cheek, my shaking didn't stop, but it slowed down.

"Load your weight upon my shoulder / I won't break 'cause I can take it," he said.

"I'm not sure what happened in there, but I have to forget," I said.

"*There's no turning back,*" Rad said, opening the car door and pushing in next to me.

"What if Danny finds out? I have to try and forget this. Oh God, what's happening to me? What if I *liked* it? Fuck."

Rad nodded softly. "*Something is changing inside you, and don't you know / Don't you cry tonight.*"

But I was already sobbing. I hugged Rad, feeling the steadiness of the guitar between us, solid and already tuned.

"*To kiss a girl won't change the world,*" he said.

"It could! I haven't even kissed Wendy!"

Rad sighed and strummed his guitar again, singing "*Imaginary lovers will never turn you down.*" He got out of the truck.

He was right, of course. It was what the Lesbian Collective had been trying to tell me in the bathroom. The Wendy I loved wasn't the actual, real-life Wendy. My Wendy was tough, strong, sexy and solitary. Not a bitch, just someone needing me to soften her, even her out and take the hard-candy sadness out of her eyes. This was *my* truth, and still, I couldn't accept that it wasn't *the* truth.

Afraid everyone else might be right and I wrong, I clutched at Rad. He reassured me, "*If being afraid is a crime / We hang side by side.*"

Suddenly a voice from behind Rad startled me, and Rad slipped out of my hands.

"Cary, c'mon back inside, huh?" said the voice. It was Danny, talking through Rad like he wasn't there.

"Yeah, okay," I said.

Rad eased out of the way and back across the parking lot while Danny took my arm and helped me out of the truck.

"See, it's just another simple twist of fate," Rad called back to me as Danny put his arm around my shoulders and kissed my neck, leading me back to the club.

Yes, I thought, it's fate. Fate for me to be with Danny now, and later . . . later maybe fate would make things different. I'd have to wait and see.

Chapter

10

"SHIT," DANNY SAID WHEN WE GOT TO THE REGISTER AT THE front of the lunch line. Digging through his pockets, he said, "I forgot my lunch card."

He flung his ponytail back and smiled at the cashier, who only stared at him with eyes hooded by false eyelashes and adjusted the pink paper cap on her head. Danny picked up a french fry and sucked on it like a cigarette.

"I got it," I said, and dropped bills onto the counter.

"You didn't have to do that," Danny said as we headed toward his table. "She would've let me go by."

"Uh-huh," I said. She never had before—I always paid. Which was okay because I had an allowance of fifty dollars a week, and I never even ate the lunch the housekeeper packed for me. Unless it was party leftovers, because I liked nibbling on caviar and crumbly crackers.

Rachel was seated at the end of the bench. When Danny started to sit down, and me next to him, she reluctantly got up and moved across the table. It didn't bother me that she was always trying to get close to Danny because I knew she wasn't real competition. Anyway, she was Jen's friend, so I was always nice to her.

"Raven! Over here!" Rachel called out to a girl who was wandering through the rows of tables. It was the girl who'd stood up to my mother at the school board meeting. "Raven's new here," Rachel said. "She just moved from Texas. She's in my homeroom."

The new girl was also in my calculus class. She'd sat in the empty seat next to Wendy which I'd been hoping to move into, once I got the guts. So now I couldn't help pursing my lips, a little angry. True, she'd impressed me at the school board meeting, but now that she was actually enrolled at school and interfering with my life—even if she didn't mean to—I was pissed.

Besides, the way she looked at me in class, and the way she kept showing up everywhere I was, I wasn't so sure she didn't mean to interfere. Ever since she had talked back to my mother, she was a constant reminder of how wimpy *I* was. She was almost like Rad, except everyone could see and hear *her*. And I couldn't make her conveniently disappear.

"I thought everyone from the South was named Mary Jane or Susie-Lou or something," I said to Raven as she set her tray down.

When Raven blushed I felt bad. "We're from the city," she said with a dainty drawl.

"Don't pay attention to Cary," Danny said, "She's still fucked-up from a bad trip she had over the weekend. I keep telling her she should eat some meat before she does drugs."

When Danny smiled at Raven, I felt myself go stiff.

What, was *she* going to move in on him, too? Then I saw that he wasn't looking at her anymore, and she wasn't looking at him at all, she was staring at me. Uncomfortable, I glanced around the cafeteria. I had to admit, she had a pretty voice, and she didn't look like a country bumpkin. Out of the corner of my eye I watched her. Her makeup was elegantly sparse and perfectly applied in shades of lavender, with plum liner outlining her neat lips. Her cheekbones were high, her chin slightly pointed, and she had straight, blue-black hair with two small corkscrew curls falling over her cheeks. In class earlier, I'd been mesmerized by her cool stockings, which had bright-colored playing cards, dice and roulette wheels spinning around her skinny legs like a living casino.

"Cary's excellent in math," Rachel said. "I bet she could help you with your calculus."

"Mr. Curry's really nice, but I feel funny asking for help on my first day. He might think I'm stupid. I wish we'd moved here right at the start of the year. I feel so far behind," Raven said.

"I guess I could help you," I said. "When do you have study hall?"

"Maybe we could go to the library after school?" she asked, raising her thin eyebrows in a way that I couldn't help liking, even if she was annoying me. Yeah, it was cute how she fluttered her lashes at me. But she wasn't Wendy.

Twisting Danny's ponytail around my fingers, I said, "Danny and I have plans for after school." I kissed his ear for emphasis.

Danny smiled at me and said, "Why don't you help her now? I don't mind."

You don't mind about anything, I thought as I shrugged and moved with Raven to a free table. She followed me like an eager puppy. Again, I both liked it and was annoyed. As we passed the window where the Lesbian Collective sat, I felt them watching us, and I put Raven between them and me.

"There's room there," Raven said, gesturing at the end of the lesbian table.

"Not enough," I said. No way was I going to encourage that group. I wondered if they all knew about Deena kissing me. How did I get to be their charity case?

She shrugged. "They're looking at you, you know."

"That's because they're weird," I said, pulling Raven to another table. Pretty soon they'd be raising funds selling "Save Cary" T-shirts.

"Why are they weird?" Raven asked. "Just because they're looking at you?"

"Just forget it. God, what's your problem? You don't even know me!"

When Raven stared at me, hurt, I softened. She was new. She wouldn't know anything yet. They probably didn't even have lesbians in Texas. Blowing at the wisps of hair in my eyes, I said, "Let's get started on the math, okay?"

We began to go over an equation, when we were interrupted.

"Raven, what's up?" said the boy who'd been slouching in the seat next to Raven and her mother at the meeting. He had bright eyes which were barely visible under his black bangs, but you couldn't help noticing them anyway. They were deep blue, like his sister's.

"This is Adam," Raven said. "Adam, Cary."

"Hey," he said, slumping into a seat. He wore a huge Dallas Cowboys shirt over sagging jeans. He couldn't have been more than twelve, but he had an attitude that was old, too old for his face. It reminded me of a lot of the junior high kids here. Babylon was small, so there was only one school for junior and senior high. The younger kids were always trying to act like they fit in with the older kids. I was the same way when I was in seventh and eighth grade.

"Why aren't you sitting with your friends?" Raven asked, ruffling Adam's hair.

He pushed her hand away. "Cut it out. I'm not a baby!" he said. "Is everyone here a snob?" he asked me.

"Adam!" Raven said. "You're not even trying."

"I don't want to," he said. "Why can't I hang around with you? Cary doesn't mind, right?"

Oh, great, I thought. I really need this.

"Cary and I are trying to study," Raven said.

"Hey, Cary," Adam said, like we were buddies already, "there's a bunch of girls checking you out. You a dyke?"

I almost died. I couldn't even talk.

"Adam!"

He stared hard at Raven for a second and then said casually, "It's not like I've got a problem with it. Girls and girls are okay. I never bugged you about—"

"Adam, enough."

"All I'm saying is I'm glad there's no *guys* staring at *me*! Gross!"

"Adam, what people do in private is their own business," Raven said.

"Whatever. I'm just saying."

"We heard you. Let me do some work now. We'll talk later."

Adam rolled his eyes and shuffled off.

Raven picked up her pencil again and began scribbling furiously, but I interrupted.

"If he didn't look just like you, I'd never guess you were related. You fight all the time?" I asked.

"Adam lived with my father until last year. He's had some problems. . . . Forget about it."

"I'm just surprised . . . since you and your mother were so outspoken at the meeting last week." I was curious, especially after what Adam had started to say about "girls and girls." But I couldn't just ask straight out.

Raven gently put down her pencil and looked me in the eyes. I couldn't move. I was mesmerized, like I had been at the school board meeting. "I believe everyone has the right to be in love," she said, "and if two people are happy together, that's all that matters. However, Adam hasn't had a lot of experience with love yet."

We worked on calculus again, until I glanced over Raven's shoulder and saw the Lesbian Collective smirking in our direction. I put down my pen.

"What about them?" I asked, gesturing. "They're not just two people in love. They're a group, making a big

64

show, trying to get everyone to think like them. You think that's okay?"

"You kiss Danny in the middle of the cafeteria, and I've seen you holding hands in the hall. You sit at a lunch table with all your friends. What's the difference?"

"I don't know," I said. "It just is."

Raven smiled, maybe teasing me, "You make a bigger show of being Danny's girlfriend than any of those girls make of their relationships. You really want to get into this now? We just met."

I was blushing. "We're not going to finish if we don't get to work," I said.

Raven looked me in the eye. "I thought so," she said.

I stared down at my book but couldn't focus because my cheeks were hot and my eyes blurry with almost-tears. Who the hell did Raven think she was, egging me on, making fun of my relationship with Danny?

Biting my lower lip, I said, "What do you know, anyway?"

"About what?" Raven asked, all innocent-like.

"About *anything*. You just moved here. How do you know what those girls are like?"

"Then why ask me?"

Raven was so smug, I wanted to smack her. Except that she was right. I was asking because it *did* seem like she knew—a lot. Maybe it was because she was new that she could see everything and everyone so clearly. She could be objective.

But it was still weird, the way she picked me, out of everyone. Even as I helped *her* with the calculus homework, *I* felt like a charity case. It was the same way the

65

Lesbian Collective had made me feel before, and I didn't like it.

Raven and I went back to work, but I couldn't concentrate on what we were doing. Thoughts were racing through my head. I hoped the school wouldn't start teaching gay history. It was embarrassing, and nobody's business anyway. And I didn't want to be gay for the world. I only wanted Wendy. I might be a little confused, maybe even a lot, but couldn't I please be screwed up in peace? I was sorry I started the whole stupid conversation.

Chapter

11

"HI, CARY." IT WAS DEENA, THE GIRL WHO HAD KISSED ME AT Phantasie.

She was on the front steps of the school, smoking a cigarette. I ignored her as Danny and I passed by. Turning up the collar on my coat, I slid my hand into the back pocket of Danny's jeans.

"You know her?" Danny asked.

"No," I said.

Instantly, I felt guilty. My throat felt like it was closing up. Pushing down the memory of kissing Deena, I kissed Danny on the lips and tried to focus on something we'd done together that was really fun, something that proved I really loved him.

Like the time we first met, last winter. I'd tripped on the hem of one of my long skirts and slid down the school steps on my butt. Danny helped me up and didn't let anyone dare laugh at me. Then there was the first time we kissed, sitting on the floor of his living room, leaning against the couch and watching a stupid TV show. I had slid my hand onto his knee, and he'd leaned in and kissed me so hard, for so long, my lips were swollen the next day. He was the best I'd ever kissed—much better than Deena!

But now, sitting on the edge of Danny's bed and waiting for him to finish smoking and kiss me, I found it hard to recapture that same thrill. Now the kisses were wet and sloppy, thick with tongue and bristly with beard stubble. Danny put out his cigarette, let loose his hair and sat next to me on the bed. As he lifted my legs up onto his lap, I wiped my lipstick off with a tissue.

"I love you," I said into his hair.

"You're beautiful," he said, stroking my arm and making the hairs stand on end. "I love you, too."

Snuggling and hugging, I could believe in anything. Danny and I were meant to be together. Nothing else mattered. I would stop doing drugs, and maybe then I'd stop feeling so weird. Maybe the drugs were the problem all along, even though they made me feel good.

A door slammed downstairs as Danny was pushing his hand into my bra. Although I tried to keep kissing, I was listening to the footsteps coming upstairs. I nudged Danny's hands away.

"It's only Wendy," he said.

I know, I thought, as Danny's bedroom door swung open. Grabbing a pillow, I put it in front of me. Wendy sauntered in, looked at us for a second, and then went to the dresser.

"Wendy! Fuck!" Danny said. "You could *knock*!"

"You could lock your door," she said, fumbling through the clutter in Danny's top drawer.

"You *broke* it," he said. "Get out!"

"Where the hell is your stash?" she said, "What'd you do, hide it?"

"I knew you were stealing from me," he said, getting up. Going to the dresser, he pulled her hands out of the drawer and said, "I told you to get out of my room. I don't go searching through your stuff."

Wendy laughed. "Whatever. Anyway, just give me one joint." Reaching into her pocket, she pulled out a dollar. "Come on. I'll pay for it, okay?"

I blushed at the way the denim of her tight jeans moved against her skin as she hooked her fingers into the belt loops. She and Danny stared at each other. Finally he sighed, went to his closet and pulled a little bag out of a Doc Martens boot. Pinching out some weed, he dropped it into Wendy's open palm, and she stalked out. By the time Danny got back to the bed, I was shaking inside.

As he leaned over me, I could hear Wendy's door shutting down the hall, and I couldn't relax. Closing my eyes, I put my hands on his waist and imagined it was hers. As I kissed his ears, I pretended I was seducing Wendy. Finally, for a minute, I felt passionate. But Danny's penis was pressing against me and making it hard to focus.

"I love you," he said, with such sincerity I couldn't stand it anymore.

"You know what?" I said, sitting up and trying to act natural. "I have to go. I'm meeting my cousin, to see her horse."

I felt bad using Jen to lie, but I had to say something besides "I don't want to have sex with you. I'm grossed out."

"So," Danny said, stroking me, "you'll be a little late."

But it was more than not wanting to have sex with Danny. It was knowing Wendy might hear us, or even walk in again. Somewhere in my mind I believed she was secretly in love with me, and if I had sex with Danny it would hurt her feelings. I felt like by having sex with Danny while she was home, I was cheating on her.

"I really have to go. I'm sorry, okay?" I said.

"Fine," Danny said, getting up and turning away.

He was mad, but I knew he wasn't going to break up with me or anything over this, so I put my shoes on. When I kissed him goodbye, he was stiff. I felt guilty again. I had to get out of there.

"I'll call you later," I said as I left. "Or maybe I'll see you tonight. Are you helping out with refreshments at parent-teacher night? I'll be there. Jen talked me into it."

Danny shrugged like it didn't matter but said, "Yeah. Mr. D said I have to if I don't want an F in gym. You know his bullshit."

"At least we'll see each other tonight," I said, trying to sound perky.

"Right." Danny didn't walk me downstairs. In the hall I looked at Wendy's door for just a second before hurrying away.

• • •

While I was walking home, Rad appeared. "I can't go on like this," I told him. "It's fucking me up. I have to forget about Wendy."

Rad tugged on his knit hat, pulling it over his red ears so only his hoop earrings showed. *You're just an empty cage, girl, if you kill the bird,* he said.

70

"I'm not killing anything real, only a love I made up. Danny's the real thing. I *have* Danny, and I love him. I thought I could love two people, but this is too hard. I owe it to Danny to remember how to love him."

"Your truth will always break it," said Rad.

"Nothing's going to break up my relationship with Danny if I don't let it. Anyway, what do you know about truth?"

"Knowledge of the universe is fed into my mind."

Angrily I said, "Maybe of the universe, but not of me. I can do anything I want. I don't have to care about Wendy. I'm forgetting already."

Rad sighed. *"Your cheating heart will tell on you."*

There were tears gathering in my eyes now, and on top of everything it was starting to rain. Cold, wet drops were making my bangs heavy and my wool coat smelly. The water made puddles in the bony curves of Rad's shoulders.

"I'm not gay, okay?" I said as we cut through the bank parking lot to my street. "What happened at Phantasie didn't mean anything, and neither did today. I just have to think."

"Everything counts in large amounts," Rad said. He wasn't even looking at me—like *he* was mad at *me* or something! He had no right.

Frustrated, I said, "First you tell me kissing Deena's no big thing, now suddenly everything matters. Why can't you make up your mind? How am I supposed to know when to listen to you if you keep talking in riddles I don't get anyway?"

"Would you mind a reflecting sign / That shows you what's

71

in your mind?" Rad asked, stopping when we reached my driveway. He kicked at the gravel with his toe.

"Just leave me alone!" I yelled, wiping at the rain and my tears. "You're not helping! I can figure this out on my own, thank you. I know what I want, okay?"

Rad's guitar looked like it was warping in the wet. He took a couple steps back. For the first time since I'd known him, he looked angry. With his lips pursed tightly he said, *"You can go your own way / You can call it another lonely day."*

"Believe me, I won't be lonely," I said. "I'll be glad to be free of you, so I can think straight."

"Freedom is just another word for nothing left to lose," Rad said as I turned away.

"Okay, Mr. Philosopher, whatever. I'll see you around—unless I'm lucky," I said, flushing with major, fuck-you-all anger. "If everyone would just leave me alone, I wouldn't have these problems."

Of course, maybe they would if I'd stop asking so many questions. I was the one who had to learn to shut up.

Chapter

12

JEN WAS ALREADY AT THE REFRESHMENT TABLE IN THE cafeteria when I arrived with my parents. My father grabbed a handful of chocolate chip cookies and led my mother briskly down the hall to the first teacher meeting. I was sulking as I joined Jen behind the table. I wanted everyone to know I was hurting.

"Cary, hold these cups while I pour," Jen said, hoisting a big jug of grape juice. "What's wrong?" she asked when I shuffled over, gloomy-faced.

I only shrugged. I might have wanted everyone to know I felt bad, but I didn't want to tell anyone why. They might talk me out of it, like Rad had tried to do. If I couldn't have Wendy, at least I could have my misery. It would prove not just that I had loved her, but also that I had inner strength. I could handle being sad without going off the deep end. I could be alone, if that's what it took.

I did not want to be gay. I'd rather be alone.

"Hi. What can I do?"

I slowly turned my head, feeling the heaviness of my aching, lovesick body, and saw, of course, Raven. I was glad to see her in a way, especially now that I'd blown off Rad. There was something comforting about Raven—her funky, flamboyant clothes and the quiet that seemed to float around her. Being near her was a little like stepping into a warm bath. When she got close, I noticed that she even smelled like soap bubbles.

Jen extended her hand. "I'm Jen," she said. "You're Raven, right? You can stack some brownies on that platter. Cary, get out the napkins. Rachel! Good, you're here, start opening up another table. Get those guys to help you. Right. Okay, everyone, let's get busy!"

Jen continued shouting orders, smiling the whole time.

"Is she your friend?" Raven asked.

"My cousin. Yeah, I guess she's my friend, too."

"She's nice. I like her," Raven said, brushing a shiny strand of hair behind her ear with a fingertip.

"You do?" I said.

Raven stopped stacking brownies for a second and took one off the top to munch on. Crumbs tumbled over her psychedelic ruffled blouse. She patted them off with tiny hands. Her fingernails were painted deep, sparkling purple.

"Yeah, what's not to like?" she said.

"I don't know," I said. "Nothing, I always thought. But that's because I know her. Sometimes her being so normal and happy all the time scares people, I think."

"Does it scare you?" Raven asked.

"Hey! Don't eat those, they're for the parents!" Jen said, hurrying past us to do some more organizing. Her hair was tied back in an efficient ponytail which bounced

emphatically with each order she gave, turning every de-
mand into a friendly request.

"I don't know," I answered Raven. "Not really, except
that it's weird that we grew up together but we're so different. I'm not sure how that happened. It makes me sad
that maybe I can't talk to her as much as I used to."

"You probably can."

"Maybe," I said. "Hey, I'll see you later. I'm going to
set up some chairs."

I slunk out from behind the table, glancing furtively
around to see if maybe Wendy or Danny had shown up. I
didn't want to see them. But if they were here, I wanted
them to see how unhappy I was—not that it mattered
really. Raven grabbed a chair and opened it.

"You don't have to follow me around all the time, you
know," I said quickly.

"Sorry," Raven said, but she kept opening up more
chairs right next to me. "Why are you so upset? Is there
anything I can do?"

I stopped and turned to her. I couldn't look right into
her eyes and be mean, so I looked at her cheek when I said,
"What is it with you?"

Raven first looked angry, and then sad. I glanced at her
eyes and saw that her lower lashes were glistening. Shit, I
thought, now what? I actually was starting to like talking
to Raven, but I didn't *want* to like anything anymore.

"Do you want me to leave you alone?" she asked. "I
will if you say so. I'm not trying to change you or anything. I'm sorry if it seemed that way. Sometimes I guess I
act like a know-it-all when I'm nervous."

"Nervous?" I said, "Because of me? Why would I make you nervous?"

She shook her head. "Not you. Everybody, everything. I'm new here, remember? I'm not good in crowds, like your cousin. I just wanted a friend, and you seemed like me. I just want to fit in with someone here. It gets lonely, having only Adam to talk to."

I felt so stupid and mean. I didn't know what to say, because even though I felt bad for Raven, and basically I liked her, she still made me uncomfortable. Anyway, I reminded myself, I didn't want friends anymore. I wanted to be alone, to mourn Wendy.

Luckily, the parents came flooding in then from the classrooms for a snack break, and we had to get busy behind the tables. My parents smiled and waved from across the room. A woman in a long flowered dress, with a crocheted purse swinging from her shoulder and thick silver rings on all her fingers, extended her hand to me. Even if I hadn't recognized her from the school board meeting, her deep, piercing eyes were a dead giveaway.

"You're Raven's mother, right?" I said, shaking her hand and putting on my meeting-parents face.

"Call me Lily. And you're Cary," she said. "Raven's told me you helped her with her math. I'm so glad she's found a friend. The move was hard for her. She left someone very special behind."

"Lily!" Raven said.

"Sorry, honey. I'll go sit with the parents. Cary, is that your father? He's the district attorney, isn't he? I'll go say hello."

It was entertaining to watch my parents with Raven's

hippie-mom. Almost worth dragging myself out of the house.

"Sorry about my mother," Raven said as she gathered empty plates from the table and stuffed them into a garbage bag. "She talks too much sometimes. I guess that's where I get it from. She's trying real hard for Adam and me."

"Who was she talking about—the one you left behind, I mean? Your father?" I asked, tying the garbage bag.

Raven laughed, a short burst more like a bark. "I'll never miss my father."

"Who then? Did you have a boyfriend?" Oh God, I thought, here I go again, asking questions I probably don't want answered.

"Something like that. But we broke up a while before the move. My mother doesn't know what she's talking about."

"Maybe sometime I could set you up with one of Danny's friends." Shut up, Cary, I told myself. Why can't you just shut up?

Raven smiled. "It was a girlfriend. In Texas, I mean." She looked at my face carefully. "Sorry, didn't mean to freak you out."

"I'm not freaked out," I said. But as I started to hurry away, my skirt caught on a splinter of wood at the corner of the table and ripped. When Raven came close to check on me, tears started streaming down my face. I turned away. Clutching my torn skirt, I hurried out of the cafeteria, out of the school and into my parents' car.

Lying in the backseat, I watched a splat of bird shit drip a white streak down the window. It would've been nice, maybe, to see Rad, but I knew he wouldn't come. I was too mean to him, and anyway, I had Raven on my mind. By the time I had blocked her out, my parents were back, chirping about all the great things my teachers had said about me.

"I don't feel well," I said.

Which was true—my mouth was dry from asking too many questions. I vowed to keep away from everyone from now on. I'd just let the world flow past me. I'd keep my mouth shut.

Chapter

13

RUBBING THE END OF THE THERMOMETER QUICKLY BETWEEN MY hands the next morning, I warmed it until it said I had a fever. Then, while my mother was glancing at it, I bolted from the bed to the bathroom and tickled my throat with my finger until I threw up an orange-juice-and-toast medley.

My body wasn't really sick. But the lurking emptiness I felt inside was hardly a good enough excuse to stay home from school. I couldn't feel anything. If I could, I probably could get the courage to face Danny, and the back of Wendy's head, and even Deena. I might become Raven's friend. But I could barely even feel the crispness of the starched sheets as my mother tucked me into bed before leaving me alone.

I didn't want to read, watch TV or listen to music. I just lay in bed, staring at the ceiling as a panic gripped and released me with thrusts of sweat and heart flutters. Sometimes I had to concentrate to breathe. Sometimes I slept. But not much.

• • •

On Wednesday I was woozy from getting only a little sleep, so I sneaked some tranquilizers from my mother's bathroom and took a quarter of a ten-milligram pill every few hours, just enough to keep drifting away. Once I thought I saw Rad in the corner of my room, just as the sun was setting. He seemed to shine out of the deep orange glow that radiated through my curtains.

"I went away just when you needed me most / Filled with regret, I've come back," he said, sad-eyed and hazy.

Waving him away, I closed my eyes.

"I guess I'll just go back to my house / And make believe I'm the moon," he said.

Then the sun was gone, and with its glow Rad was, too. I was so fucked up on my mother's pills that when I opened my eyes for a second to check, I wasn't sure how long he'd been gone, how long he'd been there, or if he'd even been in my room at all. I didn't care either.

What was important to me was forgetting about Wendy. I wanted for her to disappear as easily as the sun—and Rad.

• • •

Thursday morning I took my unicorn painting off the wall and stared for a long time at my Wendy collection. There was a folded piece of paper from her calculus notebook, scribbled with notes which faded into nonsense when she'd fallen asleep in class. Tracing my finger over the ink, I pretended I could erase Wendy as easily as I could smudge her writing. For a second, bringing the page to my face, I wanted to swallow it, as if somehow that would make her a part of me. Instead I poked my finger through the soft part of a crease. I poked some more. I ripped the whole thing into a hundred pieces—a hundred exactly. I was counting carefully.

The housekeeper hardly looked at me as I slipped out of the kitchen with a metal mixing bowl. She thought I was screwy anyway. Back in my room, I peeled all my Wendy souvenirs from their sacred place on the painting's back, then dropped them into the bowl. Sprinkling the one hundred shreds of paper over the top like spice, I lit the whole thing. Even with my window open, the pungent smoke of burning hair and sweater fuzz stung my eyes. I made them stay open, loving the burn and the headache I was getting.

• • •

That night my mother brought me the cordless phone. "It's that girl Raven again. You should be nice to her, Cary. She doesn't have a father, you know."

Was that *my* problem? But I took the phone.

"What?" I said hoarsely.

"Do you want me to bring you your books?" Raven asked. "We learned a lot of new stuff in calculus today. I could show you."

"No," I said. "I'm tired, okay? I'm sorry if I was mean the other night. I wasn't feeling well."

"You want me to leave you alone?" Raven asked.

"Yes," I said.

"Okay, whatever," she said, sounding sad—and angry, too.

I hung up and went back to sleep, cradling my aching head in my palms.

• • •

I sank my face into the pink roses Danny brought me on Friday.

"Are you going to get in trouble for cutting?" I asked stupidly. Danny get in trouble? Get serious.

"Wendy wrote me a note," he said. "Want to smoke, or are you too sick?"

I almost laughed. "I'm okay," I said.

Danny and I smoked a joint on my bed, and he stroked the bump in the blanket that was my leg. Normally, Danny acted like he didn't need anyone, cool as hell. But alone with me like this he was different. He needed me. Suddenly it was clear to me why I had to love him, why I was tied to him, even when it was so painful. He was like a wounded bird when I met him, sad and skinny and lonely like me. Lately I hadn't seen that in him. He'd become strong and popular. Before, he'd been partly invisible. Now he was aloof, floating over everyone instead of just being passed by. Maybe he'd have been popular eventually anyway—that was the only reason he sold drugs, to be necessary.

Although I wasn't popular, I was kind of accepted because of Jen. Anyway, I wasn't totally on the outside, like kids who lived in Danny's neighborhood were supposed to be. Only he and Wendy had escaped the social stigma of poverty.

It was more than my money that had built Danny up. It was having me around. He really cared about me, and since he believed I loved him back, he was more than himself around me.

Now here he was in my room, looking like his wings were bent and his feathers were drying and falling off. It was increasingly clear to me how much I had changed him and made him able to become everyone's favorite Danny. To love someone and be loved back gave power. Now he was a wounded bird again. Knowing this made me want to push him off my bed, burn his face with the end of the joint, press the rose thorns into his skin, and kick him. Just keep kicking him.

"Do you think you'll be better soon?" he said. "Did you go to the doctor?"

I didn't answer because panic was rushing at me again, pounding behind my eyes.

"You look so thin. Do you want me to go get you some food?" he asked.

"I'm not hungry," I said.

"Is it me? Did I do something?"

"What, is everything about you?" I said.

Danny blinked hard. And I was suddenly so, so sorry I had hurt him. I wanted to push him out the window. I wanted to escape the responsibility.

"You look so depressed," he said, staring at me and touching my cheek. "What's wrong?"

Sighing, I let him keep touching me. At first, his fingers felt like razors, but gradually I relaxed and accepted his generosity of feeling. I let him care about me, and felt sad.

Finally I fell against him and said, "You know I love you. No matter what happens, I always will love you."

Danny held me close. He was confused, I could tell. But so was I, so I couldn't say anything to make him feel better.

"I'll always love you," he said. "What's wrong?"

"Nothing," I said. "I'll probably be back in school on Monday."

• • •

Saturday Jen called several times, but I pretended to be asleep. We were too close and I liked her too much to lie to her. She'd see it in my face anyway. It wasn't that she'd ever judged me, but I couldn't imagine telling her I was in love with my boyfriend's twin sister. Out of love now, I reminded myself, still trying to believe it.

Anyway, Jen was too normal for me now. Raven was right, Jen *did* scare me, especially when I tried to be like her. She reminded me of what I'd never be—smiles and ponytails and a breezy convertible full of laughing friends.

"When you're better, maybe you can invite Jen over for dinner," my mother said after I refused Jen's fourth phone call.

I shrugged. "I don't know," I said. "We don't hang out that much anymore. I don't know if we have that much in common."

"She's your best friend!" my mother said. "Since you were babies!"

"I'm not a baby," I said.

My mother stroked my hair—she'd become super-Mom since I'd been in bed—and said, "You need some rest. Try to sleep, honey."

• • •

Monday I ate breakfast like a normal person, except that Rad was sitting across from me in the kitchen, nibbling a piece of bacon from my plate. The housekeeper reached through him to put buttered toast next to me.

Laughing, Rad folded his goatee up into his mouth and sucked at it. *"Nobody seems to see me / Though I stand here night and noon,"* he said.

84

The housekeeper apparently couldn't hear him, either, but I was pretty sure she could hear me, so I didn't say anything until she left the room.

When she was gone, I smacked Rad's hand away from my plate, saving the last of the bacon for myself. "So, we're still friends?" I asked.

"*As sure as night is dark and day is light,*" he said, grabbing for my toast.

"What've you been doing with yourself?" I asked.

Rad pushed his chair back and loosened the belt on his pants, which were so big on him the waist looked like a tied paper bag. He turned the screws on the neck of his guitar.

"*Smokin' cigarettes and watching Captain Kangaroo,*" he sang, smiling widely and showing off his even rows of flat teeth. He licked crumbs off his lips.

I laughed. "Well, I'm glad you're back. I missed you. Believe it or not, deep down I guess I'm understanding a little of what you say. I'm not saying you're right, though. I *do* love Danny. You don't have to believe me."

"*I don't see nothing wrong / With a little bump and grind,*" Rad said.

"No, I mean I really love him. Danny's very special. Wendy's not. I know that now."

Rad pursed his lips and stared at me, considering. Finally he said, "*Only love can make it rain.*"

"That's what I mean," I said. "I wouldn't have been so depressed if I didn't love Danny. Being sick for a week proved it. It proved how much I care about him."

"*She lies and says she still loves him / Can't find a better man,*" Rad said, getting up.

85

"Please," I said, "don't start that again. Can we not argue, please?"

Shrugging and smiling, Rad said, *"I walk the line."*

"Okay then." I pushed my plate to Rad and started to get up, then paused. "Um," I said, "I was wondering, what do you think of Raven?"

"I believe in angels / Something good in everything I see," he said, finishing my eggs.

"Well, you would," I said. "But she's not an angel, not really. She wants to be my friend. She might even have a crush on me. She's gay, you know. Not that that necessarily means . . . I don't know, what do you think?"

He shrugged and smiled, teasing but serious, too. *"We'll muddle through, one day at a time,"* he said.

"I hope so," I said as I got up. I went upstairs to pack my book bag and check my makeup. Rad was cool. He just worried too much about me, and sometimes he wasn't much help. But it didn't matter because I was feeling a lot better, actually.

I was over Wendy.

Chapter

14

"WHAT'RE YOU DOING NOW?" JEN ASKED, STANDING NEXT TO my locker after school.

I stared into my neat piles of books and fingered my coat on its hook. Danny was staying late in the art room to finish a painting, and I wasn't really doing anything. But I still didn't want to be around Jen. She made me nervous.

"Hi, Cary," said Raven as she passed.

"Raven!" I said. "We're still on for today, right?"

Raven looked at me funny, but she just smiled and shrugged. I had a feeling she'd back me up on anything. Since I'd come back from being sick, she still followed me everywhere even though I'd told her on the phone to leave me alone. But it didn't bother me anymore. And it made it easier to forget about Wendy.

Raven was beautiful, like a doll. Not as decadent as Wendy, but there was something underneath her pretty figure and dark eyes that interested me. I guess she was mysterious. The Lesbian Collective stared as Raven sat next to me at lunch every day, leaning in to copy my notes, and they smirked.

Surprisingly, it didn't bug me. It felt good to think Raven might have a crush on me. It was like a slap in Wendy's face. I knew deep down Wendy wouldn't really care either way, but it was fun to pretend I was making her jealous. I told myself that the final straw, the thing that would really get me totally over Wendy, would be if I could dump her.

But for now I had to dump Jen. Even if Raven didn't like me *that* way, I was sure she'd help me escape.

"Raven and I are going to work on our calculus together," I told Jen.

Jen smiled her usual carefree smile and said, "Great, I need to return some stuff to the library. I'll walk with you guys."

Raven stood next to Jen, waiting for me to answer. When I'd been frozen for several long seconds, Raven finally said, "We're going to my house to work."

She looked at me, and I nodded with my eyes. She practically glowed. I wondered again if she just liked me as a friend, or if there was something else. For the moment I didn't care, as long as she rescued me from having to hang out with Jen.

"Well, I'll walk with you as far as the library," Jen said hesitantly.

I shrugged. "Cool," I said.

• • •

Raven was wearing purple platform shoes and a big, white, feathery-fluffy coat that made her look like a tiny pimp-doll. I was wearing tapered wool pants, black flats and a bell-shaped coat with huge buttons and a Peter Pan collar that I'd found at the thrift shop. Jen wore 501s and a turquoise ski jacket with the stub of a lift ticket from last winter still attached to the zipper. As we walked, Jen edged between Raven and me, smiling side to side at us.

"Cary, did you finish your paper for AP History yet?" Jen asked.

"I haven't even started it," I said.

"Do you want to come over Friday to work on it? You know Dad collects history books."

"I usually go to Danny's on Friday," I said.

"Oh, yeah. How about Thursday? The paper's due next week. You better get started soon."

"I don't know, I'll think about it."

"Hey, I know," Jen said, "Saturday we could go surfing, before it's way too cold. We can have dinner at my house afterward and work on our papers."

"I don't know," I started to say.

Jen grabbed Raven's arm, suddenly excited. "Do you want to go with us Saturday? Have you ever surfed?"

Raven shook her head.

"Then you have to come. I have an extra board and you can borrow my brother's wet suit. He's away at college now, so he won't even know."

"It might be too cold this weekend," I said. "It might even rain."

Jen smiled. "It's not too cold yet. Don't be a wimp. Raven, do you ride? You should come see my horse. Cary won't learn to ride, but she feeds Lucky carrots when she comes over. Do you guys want to come over later, after dinner?"

Raven was starting to look excited, like she wanted to go, and I bit my lip.

"I haven't ridden since we moved," Raven said. "What kind of horse—"

"Okay," I said, "We're here." I pointed at the library. "Raven and I really have to get to her house and start working. We'll talk later about Saturday."

"Call me tonight," Jen said.

"I'll try," I said.

"Raven, just let me know if you want to come ride Lucky. Anytime's okay."

Raven nodded as I hurried her away from Jen.

• • •

Raven lived by the docks on Shore Road. From her window I could see the couple of boats that were still in the water slapping against the pier. While Raven arranged books and notes on her bed, I stared at the water outside as it broke into tiny whitecaps.

"I'd like to try surfing," Raven said. "Are you good?"

"It'll probably be too cold this weekend," I said. "It's practically winter."

"You don't surf in winter?" she asked.

I shrugged.

"Sorry my room's a mess. I haven't unpacked everything yet."

"I like it," I said. "It must be nice to have something to concentrate on. I mean when you have nothing else to think about, you can figure out where to put your desk, or a poster, or something."

"I always have something to think about. Usually too much. Don't you?" she said.

90

"I guess," I said. "But unpacking is so concrete. You know what's going to happen when you're done."

Raven pulled at one of her curls. "Yeah," she said, looking uncertain. "How come you wanted to get away from Jen? Are you mad at her?"

I shook my head and hesitated, wondering how much to tell her. Wondering, also, how much she'd already guessed. "No," I finally said.

"Won't she get mad if you keep blowing her off?"

"Nah, she'll be okay," I said, sitting next to Raven on the bed. I stared at her. Raven had such creamy skin and pretty eyes . . .

Then I thought, This is crazy. What am I doing?

Our knees touched and Raven blushed. I moved away a little. I'd felt a spark, like I usually felt only when I was next to Wendy.

"You know what I want to do?" I quickly said, trying to blot out the fluttering I felt in my stomach and the quivering between my legs. "Cut my hair. Do you have any scissors?"

My heart was beating fast. I swallowed hard, forcing myself not to notice the scent of Raven everywhere, and the feel of her in everything, all through the room.

While Raven fumbled through a box, she said, "But your hair's so pretty! I don't know if I should. I mean I don't know if I *can* . . ."

"Like this," I said, unfolding a picture I kept in my purse. It was a scene from *Roman Holiday*—Audrey Hepburn with a sassy, short hairdo.

"You sure you want me to do this?" Raven said, fixing a towel around my neck.

I nodded and smiled. She smiled, too, and giggled.

"You're crazy," she said.

"I'm trying," I said as the scissors made their first snip.

• • •

"You're lucky to have a boyfriend," Raven said when she was almost done.

"I guess so," I said. "Can I see yet?"

"Just a little more over here," Raven said, snipping at my bangs and stepping back to examine her work. "Okay, you can look. What do you mean, you guess? Don't you love him? Everyone thinks Danny is the coolest, most gorgeous guy . . ."

I looked in the mirror and ran my fingers through my fun new style. It was perfect. "What do you think?" I asked.

"I think I did a pretty good job. It looks like the picture, don't you think so?"

"No," I said, "I mean what do you think about Danny?"

Raven blushed. "I guess . . . well, I never thought about it . . . well, not never, but not like that. I mean he's not my type, you know what I mean."

"I thought he was mine," I said. "But sometimes I think all I can do is be a mirror—you know, reflect his feelings back at himself. Maybe that's what love is. Whatever." I paused, not sure why I was getting into this with her.

Quickly I then said, "Your makeup's cool. Show me how you do your eyes."

"That's not what love is," Raven said as she got out a box of makeup, like a fisherman's tackle box, from under her bed. She cleared a space on the floor and pulled me down to sit next to her.

As she arranged a palette of colors, she said, "When you love someone, you can absorb, you can radiate, but you don't just reflect."

I laughed. "Okay, whatever. You know, you sound like a friend of mine, this guy Rad. Except he always talks in song lyrics."

"Sounds cool. He doesn't go to Babylon, does he?" Raven asked, brushing my lids with a soft layer of color.

"Sort of. It's hard to explain."

Raven didn't say anything for a second, then she blurted, "Look, it's none of my business, but what do you *see* in Wendy?"

"What are you talking about?" I said, immediately defensive and stiff.

"It seems like you have a thing for her, and—"

"Well, I don't."

"Okay. Whatever. I was only wondering. Because I don't know her that well, but excuse me for saying so, she seems like kind of a bitch."

"She's not a bitch. You're right, you don't know her that well. God, you haven't even lived here for a month."

My mouth was dry, and I could feel my face go hot and red. Tugging at my new, shorter bangs, I licked my lips.

"I'm sorry," Raven said, closing her makeup box. "It's just that I like you. You always get upset around her."

"I don't," I said, going to the window to watch the boats.

"You're upset right now."

"Because this is so stupid. I think Wendy's interesting,

okay? She's my boyfriend's sister, so I guess I have some attachment to her. I don't like people calling her names."

Raven stood next to me at the window. "I guess she is pretty."

"She's beautiful," I said.

Raven shrugged. "So are you," she said.

My shoulders tensed. "Thanks for doing my hair. It looks great," I said. "I really have to go now."

"I didn't mean to upset you," Raven said as I gathered my things.

"I'm not upset. I just have to go," I said.

I really wasn't as upset as I wanted to be. I should've been angry, but that wasn't why I had to go. Who cared if Raven dissed Wendy? What really bothered me was how attracted I was feeling to Raven. That was like *me* dissing Wendy. Apparently I wasn't totally over her yet.

Chapter

15

I stopped near my house to think. Between the library and the bank was a narrow strip of dirt and weeds, hidden by fence on either side. I scrunched into this space, protected from the wind and other people. My head felt light, and not just because most of my hair was gone. I sniffled, but I couldn't cry. I was too angry. Angry because I was scared. What exactly did Raven want from me?

Damn it! Why wouldn't everyone just leave me alone! If they'd just give me one second to think, I wouldn't have to be as mean as I had been lately. I wouldn't have to feel so guilty.

Hearing a whistle, I looked up to see Rad climbing over the fence. For once he was dressed warmly, wearing a long, wrinkled trenchcoat that covered his hands and barely left enough space for his Converse high-tops to poke out.

As he dropped to the ground and rolled toward me, tangled in his coat, I laughed. "Why didn't you come through the hole in the fence, like a normal person?" I asked.

"*I wouldn't normally do this kind of thing,*" he said.

"What are you doing here anyway?" I asked, turning away as I remembered that I hadn't been doing so well lately talking to people. I didn't want to get into another fight with Rad.

"*Didn't I, didn't I, didn't I see you crying?*" he asked.

"No," I said, wiping my nose. "I just have a cold or something. Maybe I'm sick again."

"*Warm milk, laxatives, cherry-flavored antacids,*" Rad suggested.

Laughing, I said, "Please don't tell my mother that. She's already playing nurse too hard. It's getting creepy."

Rad shrugged and spread his coat out around him so the bottom covered me, too. I leaned against him, breathing in his warmth and imagination.

"I hate when my mother does that," someone said, squirming through the hole in the fence.

It was Raven's brother, Adam. Rad faded a little, but he didn't totally disappear like he tended to do when Raven was around. Adam crawled over the dry leaves and sat near me, his knees scrunched up to his belly. He looked small, and very young for a change.

"What are you doing here?" I asked.

"This is a cool hideout," he said, looking around and nodding his head in approval. "Sometimes I like to sneak onto one of the boats at the dock at night to be alone. You ever do that?"

I shook my head. "Did you follow me here?"

"Raven was crying after you left, and she wouldn't tell me why. Did you make her cry?" Adam said, pouting and staring hard at me with those intense blue eyes.

"I didn't mean to," I said, thinking, I can't believe I'm explaining myself to a twelve-year-old.

The anger in Adam's eyes sent a chill through me, and Rad saw it too, because he whispered to me, *"You better run for your life if you can, little girl!"*

"Raven never did anything to hurt anyone. All she does is help people—she's like that. I won't let you hurt her!" Adam shouted.

"Chill out!" I said, staring at Adam's tight fists and wondering how hard a skinny little thing like him could hit. There were scars on the knuckles, so I knew he'd had some practice.

"It's lucky you're a girl," Adam said, slapping one fist into his other palm. "I caught my father making Raven cry once, and I had to rearrange his face for him."

"What'd your father do?"

Adam curled up tighter into the brittle leaves. "What I want to know is what *you* did today. Why'd you make my sister cry?"

Now I was finally feeling the tears pool in my eyes. "She comes on a little strong, that's all."

"Yeah," Adam said, flicking at his sneakers with his fingertip. "She does that to me all the time, but she wouldn't do it if she didn't care about you. That's what my mother tells me when Raven's butting into my life, confusing me and shit."

I smiled and wiped at the teardrops rolling down my cheeks.

Adam looked up, fixating on me with those eyes again. "I think maybe Raven likes you. I mean *really* likes you, you know what I mean?"

My mouth dropped open. Finally I said, "I have to get home soon," and I started to get up.

"You got a problem with that?" Adam asked. "I mean, yeah, okay, my sister's gay, okay? You got something to say about that?"

Adam had uncrouched and was up on the balls of his feet, in a miniature fighter's stance. I might've thought it was cute if I hadn't been so surprised.

"No," I said. "But I don't think it's any of your business."

"My sister's my business," he said.

"Anyway, I thought you said being gay was gross."

Ha! Got him there, didn't I! I was standing now, too, poised to fight. I couldn't believe this little kid could get me going like this.

"It's different. She's my sister."

I started through the hole in the fence.

Adam followed me. "Don't be mad," he said. "I just don't like when Raven cries."

I stopped and looked back at him, standing tall against the wind, which looked like it could blow him away. His face was red, whether from anger or the cold, I couldn't tell. I wanted to hug him, he looked so frail. For once, I didn't feel so confused. I mean, compared to Adam, I knew a lot.

Then he said, "You don't have to be her girlfriend. I know you're going out with that guy Danny. He's cool. You could just be Raven's regular friend. Raven says love isn't about sex. It's inside you, it's not what you do with another person."

Whoa, I thought, blinking my eyes quickly.

98

Adam shrugged. "You don't even have to love her," he said. "You could just be her friend. But it's not fair to make her cry. She didn't do anything bad to you. You better not do it again."

Adam's fists were clenched again, and I stepped back, not wanting to risk being hit. "I'm sorry," was all I could mumble, hurrying away.

It wasn't until I reached my driveway that I started to feel more mad than bewildered. Who did this kid think he was? I'll make my own friends, thank you. It wasn't my fault if Raven was supersensitive.

"I've learned a lot that I don't want to know," Rad said, sidling next to me.

"No kidding," I said. "You know, I have enough on my mind without some kid putting a guilt trip on me."

I put an arm around Rad's bony shoulders. "By the way, thanks for sticking around," I said. "The way things are going, you're going to be the only friend I have left."

Rad slipped a hand out of his coat sleeve and rubbed my head. *"Just take it like it comes,"* he said.

"I'm trying," I said. "I can be happy with Danny, right?"

But even as I said that, it occurred to me that Danny was hardly an issue anymore. Except that one way or another, I was going to have to break up with him. I'd been thinking about Raven more than anything lately, I realized. If there could be something worse than leaving my boyfriend for a girl, it would be leaving Wendy for another girl.

I paused at the back of my house. "I don't know what to do about Raven. I want to be friends with her, but . . ."

"If it makes you happy, it can't be that bad," Rad said.

". . . but it's pretty obvious she has a crush on me. I don't know how to handle that. And if I weren't going out with Danny, there's still Wendy."

Even as I repeated in my head that there always will be Wendy, I kept rambling on to Rad, "Okay, Raven's pretty. I like her. She smells nice. She *is* nice.

"You know, this is so stupid. I don't even know why I'm thinking about her. She has nothing to do with anything. And she's not Wendy! God, am I babbling? Why do you listen to me? You can tell me to shut up any time now. I don't know why you put up with me."

Rad shrugged and smiled. His wide mouth took up almost his whole face. *"I'm just see-through faded, superjaded, out of my mind,"* he said.

"I believe it. Maybe you should get a life, and forget about me," I said. "I'm beginning to think I'm a hopeless case anyway."

Rad shook his head.

"Thanks," I said. "It's nice having you around."

"You just call out my name, and you know wherever I am / I'll come running," Rad said as I went inside.

Chapter

16

DANNY AND I WENT TO PHANTASIE FRIDAY NIGHT, AS USUAL. A change of scenery might've been nice, but I was too self-absorbed to even suggest it. Instead, I did more drugs. A hit of Ecstasy, a joint and three gulps of vodka in Danny's truck helped me to avoid Wendy, the Lesbian Collective, and Raven. Only Raven seemed to care. She tried to dance with me, tried to talk to me in the bathroom, tried to get close to me. But I kept Danny as a wall between us, until even he was annoyed with me.

"Why are you so clingy all of a sudden?" he kept asking, trying to shrug me away. I didn't care. I danced in numbed oblivion, spinning round and round in my full taffeta skirt until I felt close to puking and far from feeling.

It wasn't just the drugs and alcohol. Being in Raven's bedroom had scared me, and I swallowed all my feelings like oysters, raw and slippery, without chewing first. Just let my emotions go down into my gut, not tasting them.

Of course, the drugs did help.

• • •

Saturday my parents were up early, rummaging around, looking for their golf equipment. It woke me up, and I went into my father's den, leaned back in his desk chair and stared at the darkly paneled wall. I still felt trippy from the night before, and the wood grains seemed to shift into roads and paths as I watched. When they didn't seem to lead anywhere tangible, I turned away and moved to the couch, zoning in on the blank TV screen set into the wall. Wiggling my feet, I pretended the bunny heads on my slippers were chattering at me.

But it wasn't the bunnies. It was my mother. "Honey," she said, "we're off to the club. Be sure to eat something today."

"Isn't it cold for golf?" I asked.

"I think we can squeeze another eighteen holes into this season," my father said. He adjusted the brim of his cap over his distinguished white hair and smiled his big politician's smile. It was habit for him. He couldn't help it.

I didn't grin back, but I managed to say, "Have fun."

"Are you sure you're feeling all right?" my mother asked as she stared at a golf ball in her hand, rubbing it with her thumb. "I can stay home with you if—"

"I'm fine," I said. "I just need a nap."

And I *was* fine, except for a blurring hangover. Actually, the hangover made me feel even more fine. The thudding behind my eyes was something to concentrate on. If I puked, it would only be yellow phlegmy stuff, not thoughts, not worries about Raven or Wendy. I only had the strength to focus on one person, Danny, who I'd had sex with behind the garage last night, with my mother's stupid chickens pecking at my feet. And it wasn't that bad, like it never was. If it was true you could have love without sex, then you could also have sex without love. It wasn't all that great, but it wasn't horrible.

After a while, the housekeeper came in with the vacuum, ruining my concentration on the blank TV, so I moved back up to my room. I didn't even realize I'd fallen asleep until the phone woke me up.

"Where have you been all day?" Jen said—too loudly, I thought. "It's getting late. I'm coming over now to get you."

"I was sleeping," I said.

"It's like three o'clock!" Jen said, laughing. In my head, I could picture her flinging her brown curls away from her face, and then maybe taking a sip from a Diet Coke.

"I don't know if I feel like surfing today," I said.

It seemed like a long time before Jen answered. When she did speak, I was surprised at the tone of her voice. I couldn't remember Jen ever sounding anything but chipper since we were kids.

"I don't know what I did wrong," she said, "but I'd rather you talked to me about it than keep on acting like this."

"Like what?" I asked, trying to sound carefree.

Jen was quiet, and I knew she was biting her fingernails. "It's like you don't want to be around me anymore. I don't get it. I know I don't go out partying with you, and maybe I'm a little dull for you, but you don't have to completely blow me off all the time."

Now I shrank back into my pillows, feeling so bad I thought I was going to cry. I shook my head, frenzied, trying to get the hangover headache back so I could feel

103

bad about myself, not Jen. I couldn't believe I actually had the power to piss Jen off, even hurt her feelings. It was too much responsibility.

Forcing myself to smile, as if she could see me, I said, "I haven't been blowing you off. I'm really sorry if it seemed that way. I just haven't been feeling that well. I'm getting up now. I'll be ready in half an hour, okay?"

"Yeah," she said, peppy again. "I'll see you soon."

• • •

I wasn't feeling guilty anymore after Jen picked me up. Raven was with Jen and got out of the car to move into the backseat. I was angry. I felt like I was being ganged up on. Although she'd invited Raven the other day, Jen hadn't told me this morning that she was coming. Good thing Adam wasn't there, too, or I would've had to leave.

"This is so cool," Raven said. "I hope I do okay. I've never been in the ocean before."

"Just don't take any advice from Cary," Jen said, "and you'll be okay."

I stared out the window, wishing for once that Danny was there. At least he made sense. At least I could hide behind him.

"I'm only kidding," Jen said, slapping me on the arm. Then to Raven she said, "Cary's a pretty good surfer, actually. Although she's gotten a little out of practice."

• • •

I still didn't feel like talking when we got to the beach. As we trudged through the sand, I focused on the waves in front of me. My feet felt tight and cramped in their neoprene booties, but I knew it was too cold to go barefoot and getting colder as the sun dropped against the horizon and the wind got stronger.

"I feel so funny," Raven said, tugging at the wrinkles in her borrowed wet suit. "Maybe I should've rented a suit my size. Do I look stupid?"

"What's the difference? Who are you trying to impress?" I said, wading into the water.

Raven looked hurt, but I didn't care. What'd she want me to say, that she looked like more suit than person, and yes, she did look stupid? While Jen started coaching Raven on how to catch a wave, I pushed ahead into the water, gripping my board tightly. Chills ran through me as the water got deeper and curled inside my suit. It felt good when my fingertips started to tingle sharply because I knew that soon they'd be numb, like *I* wanted to be, through and through. Not caring about anyone or anything—just like Wendy.

I caught the first good wave in, and even though the surf was rough, I didn't tumble off my board until I had almost reached the shore. I saw Raven struggling and sputtering as a wave knocked her down. I almost went to help her, but Jen got there first. Fuck it, I thought, and headed back out to sea.

After an hour Raven had given up and was sitting on the shore, watching and cheering whenever Jen or I came gliding in. I was getting tired, and a little cold, but I didn't want to be alone on the beach with Raven in the oncoming darkness, so I followed Jen out again for a final run.

As I paddled out, I started to think, I'm glad I came. The ocean always made me feel healed. Gradually, as water splashed over me, I was even glad Raven had come, and it was good to be around Jen again. The sun was setting, and I rested on my board for a minute, watching Jen catch a wave in and then staring at the sun to see if there really would be a green flash after it had gone down. I didn't see green, but after the ball of red had disappeared, the sky glowed purple and orange over the shore, and I thought, this is so cool. I'd never been surfing at dusk before.

With all my thinking, and examining the beauty of the sky, and starting to feel sentimental and shit, I didn't notice I was drifting. When I tried to catch a wave, I realized my positioning was way off. The next wave crashed on top of me, and I lost hold of my board. It spun in the surf, pulling at the cord attached to my ankle and wrenching my leg into painful contortions.

By the time I surfaced again, I could see another big wave coming down on me. Although I grabbed frantically for my board, my fingers were stiff with cold and slipped off before I could pull it under me. Again I was tossed under the surf, and the board's tugging and tearing at my ankle made it worse. I couldn't fight my way up with the tide pulling my leg under and out. As salt water shot up my nose, I reached down to undo the Velcro strap tethering me. Forget the board, I thought. Before letting it go though, I remembered it was a flotation device. I might need it later. A lot like Danny.

By the time I surfaced again, I was gasping for air and thinking, where the hell is the *Baywatch* crew when you need them? I want David Hasselhoff, and I want him now!

I got back onto my board and was paddling as hard as

my cold hands and tired body could when the next wave hit. But I didn't even try to catch it—I was too panicked about the riptide that was dragging me out more than in. The wave knocked me off the board again, and I thought, just when the day was starting to get good, I'm fucking drowning. This sucks.

The next time I regained control of my board, I tried to look toward the shore but couldn't see it anymore. Stars had come out, but they didn't make the ocean seem any smaller, or less black. There was a lull in the wave action, so I relaxed, trying to catch my breath. As the tide yanked me out to sea, I thought, there's a reef out there. How far could I go? I probably won't die, if I can stay on my board. I was glad I hadn't set it free before. The sky was studded with so many stars, I couldn't decide which one to wish on. And my head was so salt-water-clogged, I didn't know what to wish for.

"I've often tried to hold the sea / The sun, the fields, the tide," said a familiar voice that would've scared the crap out of me if the ocean hadn't already done that. Rad's head popped up out of the darkness, salty-wet and blue-cold, but absolutely calm. I could barely see him. Maybe I was already dead.

"Am I dead? Did I drown?" I asked. "I know I'm caught in a bad riptide or something."

"It's full speed baby / In the wrong direction," Rad said before ducking under. When he surfaced, he was holding onto the end of my board. A wave crashed over us, and I knew I couldn't be dead or it wouldn't have hurt so much when the surfboard hit me in the head. My legs and Rad's tangled together underwater, and even when my hands let

go, he kept hold of my board. When I forced my head up out of the water again, Rad was already on top of the surfboard. He was wearing regular clothes and, of course, his Converse high-tops. His torn jeans hung over his bony legs in heavy, wet folds, and his knit hat was wrapped in seaweed.

"Hold on, hold on, hold on to me," he said, not looking at me but staring ahead at where the shore must be.

I climbed on top of him and wrapped my arms tightly around his slim torso just as the next wave hit. Just hold on, I told myself as we tumbled under water. Keeping my eyes shut, I put all my energy into continuing to hold on, no matter what, as the waves kept pummeling us. I didn't even notice at first when my feet were dragging in the sand on the shore.

Opening my eyes, I tried to stand, but I was too cold and shaky, so I sank down to the sand and looked around for Rad. I hadn't even felt him crawl out from under me, and now it was too dark to see where he might have gone.

"Cary!" I heard. Jen and Raven were running toward me, flapping their arms.

"Oh my God," Raven said. "I thought you were dead! I kept looking for you, but it was too dark to see . . ." She hugged me, and I let her, I was so happy to be on land again.

"I started to go out to look for you," Jen said, joining in the hug, "but it was so dark. I didn't think it would do any good for us both to be stuck out there. Are you okay?"

"We were just going to call the Coast Guard or something," Raven said.

"I don't know what happened," I said, letting them help me up. "It got dark so fast. I panicked, I guess."

Jen carried my board, and Raven rubbed my hands as we walked. As the numbness disappeared, I felt my fingers tingle and hurt again, and that was okay.

Chapter

17

THE TIME PASSED QUICKLY THROUGH THANKSGIVING AND Christmas. I was too dazed by life to pay much attention to it. I willed everything to be normal, like it was at the beach with Jen and Raven—except, of course, for the almost-drowning thing. I asked my father for a raise in my allowance, and I started buying an eighth of pot from Danny every week. I smoked several times a day to keep feeling comfortable with myself.

Just rolling a joint felt good. I liked breaking the dirt-green bud into teensy bits and gently removing stray seeds. The finished skinny white stem was my own creation, and deciding to smoke it was so easy. So unlike making decisions about life. The fuzzy burn in my mouth led to swimmy dreams where everything went right. I could smile behind glossy eyes and not have to make any decisions in the real world. And drugs made Danny appear beautiful.

Once, after slipping my money into his pocket, he said to me, "You don't have to buy it. I'll give it to you. You *are* my girlfriend."

But I didn't want to owe him more than I did already.

• • •

One day I was in the bathroom, not sneaking a joint as usual but just peeing. Some girls came in and were talking by the mirror.

"I swear, if she doesn't keep away from David, I'm going to fucking kill her!" one said.

"That would be nice," said someone else. "She's such a slut. What is her problem?"

Who? I wondered, although I had a pretty good idea and it made my stomach cramp.

"I wish her brother was as slutty as her," the first girl said, laughing.

"Really. I mean is Danny hot or what?" said the other girl. "Man, I would do him upside down and backwards!"

"I saw him with his shirt off in gym class the other day."

"Can you believe he's still going out with that weird girl?"

That would be me, I thought. Then I couldn't help thinking, I'm weird and Wendy's a slut—we're meant for each other.

"What is up with that makeup and the hair?"

"At least it's not all pinned up like before. I mean I could see if she wore a pair of jeans and a nice shirt, she might look okay."

"She's so skinny!"

I looked at my arms, which were skinny, it was true. I didn't eat much. I didn't like to eat. I liked being skinny.

Fuck them, I thought, because they're not the ones fucking Danny!

I waited to hear if they had any more to say about me, or Wendy, but they left the bathroom. For a while I sat on the toilet trying to pee, feeling my bladder full but too tense to squeeze anything out. So I lit a roach I found in my wallet, not caring when the bell rang, not caring if I was late, or if I got caught, even though my parents would freak if I got suspended. I was getting more reckless and it didn't matter. Life was becoming fuzzy swimmy sweet. So this was how Wendy did it, the aloofness.

• • •

I wasn't going to let those girls get a chance at Danny. When we went to his house on Friday after school, I climbed on top of him. I shook, shivered and moaned, "Danny, I love you."

"I love when you say my name," he said.

I said it again and made a point of saying it often, to myself as much as to him, like a reminder of how much I cared about him.

I said it while I waited for him by his locker after school, hurrying to be there before him. I said it while I clutched his hand, walking the hallways or shivering under the bleachers outside. I was totally committed and kept my eyes down in calculus class, never looking at Wendy.

Raven and I stayed friends. We didn't talk about love. If she got a milk mustache on her upper lip and I wiped it off, my fingers pausing for just a second, and it seemed like that whole business of, you know, might come up, I would ask quickly if Adam was finally adjusting to life in Babylon. Just like that, the subject was changed. Raven listened when I babbled, high and giggly, about Danny reaching under my blouse at the movies, and how I had lost a button. She went to Phantasie and dazzled Danny's friends with tiny skirts, sparkly silver go-go boots and body glitter. In the flashing strobe lights, dancing in spinning circles, she reminded me of Rad, but more real. *Her* glitter could rub off on you if you brushed against her.

• • •

Through Christmas I continued to be the best girlfriend Danny could have. I walked with him everywhere. I was enthusiastic when we had sex. I was nice to his friends.

Christmas Eve I went into the city with Raven. It was my first time totally away from Danny in weeks, it seemed, even though I'd been to Jen's house for dinner a couple times, and Raven and I had studied together a lot. On the train I started to massage the soreness that had been lodged in my shoulder for months. I realized suddenly that the spike of pain was gone. I felt really good sitting next to Raven, breathing in her lavender perfume.

We took a cab to the East Village and ate vegetarian food at DoJo's on St. Marks. Afterward, we walked around.

"Ooh," she said, pulling me into a hole of a store. She rested her finger against a unicorn pendant, and I wondered how she'd noticed it. It was almost lost in a jumbled display of pot leaves and Harley symbols, with a few dragon claws and crystals dangling from black cords.

"I love unicorns," she said.

"I have a painting of one over my bed," I said.

"Really? I'd like to see it sometime. Maybe I could come over tonight?"

Maybe, I thought. Then I remembered how normal everything was starting to be. Just because her hand felt good in mine didn't mean I was going to change my life. Letting her into my room would be too much. I might do something I'd regret.

"I'm seeing Danny tonight. You know, it's Christmas Eve and all. I have to give him his presents."

"Oh yeah, right," Raven said.

She shrugged, like it didn't matter that I never invited her over to my house. I think it was partly Danny's influence—you only invite someone over if you're planning to have sex. Not wanting to think about that again, I started to tell her a Danny story. But she didn't look like she was in the mood, so I shut up. I didn't want to rub it in that she didn't have anyone special for Christmas. Or that I was still seeing Danny, when I shouldn't be.

So when we left the store, we didn't talk for a while. We hardly talked the whole way home. I held the package containing a leather jacket for Danny tightly to my chest, unwilling to feel guilty. It wasn't my fault Raven didn't have a girlfriend. Adam couldn't accuse me of making her cry this time.

Snow blew past the window of the train and I stared out at it, feeling like the flakes were fluttering through me. I wished I could make Raven understand how much I had invested in Danny, and even though it might only be in my head, in Wendy. I'd only known Raven for a few months. I couldn't give her more than I gave them. I had to distribute my feelings according to how much I owed people if I was going to maintain my life as I knew it.

But glancing sideways at Raven's soft skin, eggshell

white and as fragile, I felt I couldn't keep ignoring her. I wanted more of her.

Maybe if I could picture Raven with someone else, I wouldn't keep having fleeting images of us together. I wouldn't feel so defensive with Raven if she wasn't threatening the plans and decisions I was trying so hard to make. Raven gave me "the mean reds," as Audrey Hepburn called them in *Breakfast at Tiffany's*. The mean reds were like the blues, except you're so scared you shiver with anger.

"What was she like?" I asked.

"Who?"

"The girl—your girlfriend back in Texas."

"You don't have to ask me about her. I know you don't really care. You don't have to pretend," Raven said. Her voice was high pitched and shivery. She sounded like she had the mean reds, too.

"Whatever," I said, fluttering my eyelids to hold back the tears.

Confused tears, shameful tears, worried tears, because maybe Raven wasn't liking me so much anymore. I felt awful because I *wanted* her adoration, and Danny's, and, of course, Wendy's.

Everybody should love me, so in case I make a wrong choice, I have a backup.

"Kelly was the kindest person in the world," Raven said suddenly, almost to herself. "And smart, and strong. I used to be scared like you are, but even more. Kelly was soft and warm. She taught me to dream—and to love."

"You?" I said. "But you're so sure of everything."

Raven was picking at her cuticles. "Once," she said,

staring down at her hands, "after my parents were divorced, my mother was working and I fell asleep on the couch. My father sneaked in, probably looking for money as usual. I was dreaming that I was drowning facedown in a mud puddle. I woke up, and he was drooling and slobbering like a dog, all over my face."

Holding my breath, I clutched Danny's jacket to my chest. I felt horrible for ever thinking badly of my own parents.

Raven continued, "I wiggled away and ran out. Behind me, I heard Adam on the staircase, shouting like a grown man, ordering my father to leave. But I ran away, leaving Adam there all alone."

Patting Raven's knee, I tried to comfort her without getting too physical and scaring myself again. Especially now, those feelings would be wrong. Raven nudged my hand away and wiped her face with her sleeve. Two sniffles, three deep breaths and a quick shake of her head, and she was soft and calm again, the Raven I was used to.

"Anyway," she said, "when I got to Kelly's house down the block, she went right away and fetched Adam. She took care of us both until Mom got home. Kelly could do anything."

"Do you still keep in touch?"

Raven shook her head. "She's with someone else now. She's in love."

"I'm sorry. It must be hard."

Looking at me with somber eyes, Raven said, "It happens. Like with any relationship. Heteros aren't the only ones who break up, or break hearts. But just because I'm gay doesn't mean I can't move on and fall in love again with someone else."

"But if Kelly was your true love—"

"Why do you think there's only one 'true' love for everyone?"

I shrugged.

"Just because you loved someone once doesn't mean you have to tie yourself to her forever and ever."

Thank God the train pulled into the Babylon station then, because the mean reds were coming back. I had to get away, before Raven started making too much sense.

• • •

"Rad," I said as I wrapped presents that night, "why do I have so much trouble being around her? I always end up feeling guilty, or totally freaked out, but I can't stand not being around her, either."

"Isn't there something between talk and sex / Is there a place between obsession and apathy?" he said.

"That's what I want to know," I said. "Do you think Raven's there, in the in-between?"

Rad cut a length of red ribbon for me and I tied it around the neck of the bottle of perfume I got for my mother. *"Oh yeah,"* he said.

"But what is in-between? If it's not obsession, or talk, or sex, what is it?" I asked.

"A love supreme," he said.

"What if there isn't any love?" I said, swallowing hard. "What if it's all these games, and that's it? Even Raven doesn't believe in one true love!"

Rad shook his head at me so hard his Santa cap fell off.

117

"How do you know?" I asked, reaching for his hands. He wrapped his long fingers around mine and rubbed the backs of my wrists. *"I keep my eyes wide open all the time,"* he said.

"Then it's just me," I said, starting to cry. The harder I tried to be normal, it seemed the more I cried. "Am I the only one who's afraid? Maybe there's no such thing as unicorns, or angels, or fairy tales, anyway."

"Starlight and dewdrops are waiting for thee," Rad said.

I shook my head and focused on folding bright, cheerful paper around boxes. "I don't believe that," I said. "I've got to stop thinking so much. I'm driving myself crazy."

I got a joint out from under my mattress, opened the window, lit it and sucked. Rad shrugged, and we didn't talk anymore. Every now and then I'd look at him, expecting him to say something important, but he just pulled his shirt over his knees and sat curled in a ball, rocking, and looking the way I felt. Like I *still* felt despite the pot, which wasn't working for me tonight.

Chapter

18

WORD SPREAD FAST AROUND SCHOOL THAT DANNY AND Wendy were having a party on New Year's Eve. Their parents would be in Florida visiting the twins' grandparents. Even Jen was going. Danny and Wendy might live in a bad part of town, but everyone knew that's where the wildest parties were.

I got to the party late and was surprised to see Jen dancing on the coffee table with Raven. I was even more surprised at how jealous I felt. But instead of joining them, I got a beer and scanned the throbbing mass of people for Wendy. As hard as I tried, I still couldn't get Wendy completely out of my mind. Whenever I kissed Danny, I was reminded how much his nose was like Wendy's, and I wondered if their lips felt the same, soft and puckered.

Jen came up to me and leaned hard on my shoulder. She could barely stand up, and her drink smelled mostly like alcohol and very little like whatever the pink stuff in it was. I gulped at my beer, figuring I had a lot of catching up to do.

"Wow, this is fun," she said. "Brad asked me to

go to the ball at the club with him, but this is so much better!"

"Yeah," I said. "My parents went to the ball. They wanted me to go."

"I told my mother I didn't have a dress to wear," Jen said, giggling.

"I'm glad you're having a good time," I said.

"Yeah," Jen said, wobbling away.

But I wasn't glad. Jen was supposed to be my anchor. What would I hold onto if she fell down?

"Hey," Raven said. "What's up? You're so late, I was afraid you weren't coming."

"What're you drinking?" I asked, pointing at her cup.

"Ginger ale. I don't drink," she said. "I just dance. Come on!"

"I should find Danny," I said.

"I'll go with you," she said casually, like we'd never had the conversation on Christmas Eve about her ex and her father.

Raven threw her arm over my bare shoulder. As we wove through what seemed like the whole senior class, I was aware of her fine black hair brushing against me, and I didn't shake her arm off. It felt nice. Anyway, everyone was too drunk to think we were anything but just friends. We *were* just friends. Although when we passed Wendy slumped against the kitchen door, I held my head high, as if I could make her jealous. Raven smelled good, like apricots and lavender, and it scared the shit out of me.

Danny was in the basement playing poker. Raven dropped her arm as we entered, and Danny pushed the guy next to him away, clearing a milk crate for me to sit on. The table was one of those big industrial spools standing on end. The basement walls were carpeted with thick grayish red shag. Wendy's electric guitar was propped in the corner next to an amp, and I remembered the first time I was at Danny's house, sitting in the living room and listening to her play beneath me—long, sad notes and angry strumming that spoke to me. I remember it as the turning point, when my crush turned to love.

On the walls hung a collection of velvet paintings—paint-by-numbers his mother did, Danny once told me. Next to a painting of Wile E. Coyote was one of Jesus praying. It was my favorite place in Danny's house, except for Wendy's room.

"Nice dress," Danny said, kissing the shoulder where Raven's dainty hand had been. "Here."

He gave me a plastic bag of pennies, nickels and dimes to play with. Raven sat across from us, dumping change out of her purse as she was dealt into the game, too. I accepted the bong happily when it was passed to me, and sucked so deeply I coughed until my eyes watered. I felt very out of tune with everything except the velvet paintings.

● ● ●

I knew Raven was watching when Danny and I kissed at midnight, so even though I was stoned and a little drunk, I was still freaking out. I lost the rest of my money very quickly after that. By two only Raven and Danny were still playing, and it was getting vicious. As they threw dollars on top of the pile of change, I focused on Wendy, who was in the corner strumming an eerie, tuneless piece on her guitar. I was impressed by how easily she could detach herself whenever she wanted.

Suddenly Wendy stood up, just as Raven won the last of Danny's money. "Yo, Danny, 'shrooms?" she said.

"Right on," he said. Even though they fought all the time, it was sometimes so obvious they were twins. They had their own wavelength.

We went upstairs, and I was surprised to see that practically everyone had left. The floor was cluttered with cans and cups, and spilled dip had congealed on the kitchen table. The floor was scarred with cigarette burns and scuff marks. A few couples were asleep or passed out on the couch, and after Danny turned off the stereo, which was playing Live so loudly, it practically sounded like they *were* live, the house was amazingly quiet. I heard a flush, and Jen stumbled out of the bathroom, wiping her mouth and looking glassy eyed and disheveled. I couldn't believe that my anchor had just puked her guts out and was now at the kitchen table with Danny, Wendy and Raven, pawing through a bag of mushrooms.

"Jen, do you think you should?" I asked.

"Come on, Cary, let me have some fun for once. Why do I always have to be good?"

"It's just you seem pretty wasted . . ."

Jen waved her hand at me and grimaced as she chewed a mushroom stem and forced herself to swallow. "I don't have anything to do tomorrow. I can be hungover. Here, have some."

I shook my head. I felt like I was already tripping—badly. I didn't need drugs to make it worse.

Pretty soon the stereo was back on, this time playing Nine Inch Nails, which I guess was more psychedelic. Anyway, everyone seemed to be grooving. I smiled and watched them tripping, trying to be a good sport but feeling totally out of it, and a little hurt. I mean, I could pretend to laugh when they did, and I could even talk to them, but I felt invisible.

Finally I left them staring into a teapot and went back to the basement. Cards were strewn over the table, and I tried stacking them into a castle, but they kept falling down. As I refilled the bong and smoked by myself in the semidarkness, I began to feel better. Hearing stomping and laughter upstairs, I stopped playing with the cards and went back up. Everyone was sort of dancing, sort of floating, sort of pulsing, although the music had stopped. Jen was trying to spin on the floor like a break-dancer, but she kept rolling over and hitting her head against the table legs.

I leaned against the stove, watching. Eventually they slowed down. Raven was on top of the washing machine, swinging her legs against the side and staring at me, although it felt like she was looking through me. Taking my pearls off, I swung them in front of my face, trying to trip Raven out. She swayed with the motion of the necklace but other than that didn't react. Danny slid up next to me and put his tongue in my ear.

The noise, the poker game, Jen wasted, all my friends tripping—it was too much. I pushed Danny away.

"Stop," I whispered, hardly moving my lips.

"What? Why?" he said, leaning into me.

"Everyone's looking," I said, although if they were, they probably didn't care.

As Danny brushed his hair back behind his ear, I saw Wendy on the floor. She was wearing the tight pink dress I liked best on her. Now it was gathered up practically to her waist, and I could see her matching pink underwear. A chill gripped my throat, and for a second, when Danny kissed my lips, I thought it was Wendy.

But I could feel his bristly face and hands that were too big to be hers. "Not now," I said.

"What's the big deal?" he asked.

"I don't know. Just not now. There's all these people around. Jen's here."

"She's your cousin, what does she care?"

"Your sister's right there on the floor!" I said as Danny reached down the front of my strapless black dress, almost exposing a breast.

"She doesn't care. She's always making out with guys in front of me."

"You don't understand," I said.

"So explain," he said, kissing my neck.

"Forget it," I said.

I let Danny kiss me for a minute, pretending I wasn't grossed out, and then I wandered away into the living room. He didn't follow me, which was fine. I only wanted to sleep.

I woke up, who knows how long after, with a neck cramp. Wendy was making out on the couch with the guy I recognized from Phantasie, the one with the dragon tattoo. As he fingered her breast, I shut my eyes again. Although I tried to stay awake to listen, I must have fallen asleep again, because the next time I opened my eyes Wendy and the guy were gone, my leg was numb, and Jen was sitting in the corner, staring into space.

I shut my eyes, then opened them again. I was fully awake now, for the first time in months. Things had been so wrong tonight . . . it finally felt right. Right for me to make up my mind, if I could get the guts.

But when I went upstairs to Danny's room, he was curled into a ball in the corner of his bed. Brushing his hair off his face, I kissed him on the forehead. He rolled over and curled up tighter, clenched in a post-trip sleep. I climbed into bed next to him and stared at the ceiling, relieved not to have to say anything yet. By morning maybe everything would go back to how it had been, a long time ago, when things made sense. A guitar strummed gently.

"Some New Year, huh?" I said to Rad. "Do you think it's my fault Jen got so fucked up tonight?"

"Don't even worry about that song and dance," he said.

"I guess I haven't been a good friend. I just don't know what I want. It would be easier if I knew what everyone else wants from me."

Rad came close and knelt by the side of the bed, leaning his guitar against my chest. *"Some of them want to use you / Some of them want to be used by you."*

"I love Danny still, no matter what," I said, almost to myself. "Just not like he loves me."

"You're every love song ever written," Rad answered, taking off my shoes and placing them neatly next to the bed. He sounded tired.

125

"I'm sorry I don't love him enough. I still want Wendy. Raven—I can't even think about her," I said. My eyes were shut, and I was drifting away.

I could hardly feel Rad near me anymore. He must've taken his guitar back, because it wasn't on me when I rolled over to hug Danny.

As I fell asleep with the morning sunlight playing over me, Rad sang me a lullaby, *"Oo-ooh child, things are gonna get easier . . ."*

Chapter

19

It was late in January the next time I went to Phantasie. Things were still the same, despite my New Year's resolution to commit to a decision. I spent a lot of time imagining possibilities. Like Wendy breaking up with the tattooed guy she was seeing all the time now, coming into Danny's room and pulling me from his bed, declaring her love for me. My fantasy life got richer, and I still avoided reality by smoking, drinking and dropping a lot of E. So much for New Year's resolutions.

Raven was at the club, wearing vinyl pants and a shimmering gold shirt printed with faces of Marilyn Monroe. I placed her between Danny and me as I watched Wendy swivel and sway. Wendy's hair was greener than usual—a new shade. Excusing myself, I followed Wendy into the bathroom and stood next to her at the mirror.

As I wet my fingers and ran them through my hair, I watched as Wendy pulled her hair into tiny pigtails. Her hair was still short, and they poked straight out from her head, making her look like a flower fairy. She didn't look at me, even when I talked.

"I like your hair like that. It looks really cute," I said. She shrugged and penciled purple liner on her eyebrows.

"Danny told me you're getting a new band together," I said.

"Whatever," Wendy said. "Here comes your girlfriend. Why don't you talk to her."

She left, bumping into Raven as she passed.

"Do you have to follow me everywhere?" I said so loudly that everyone in the crowded bathroom looked.

"Danny sent me in to tell you he was going out to the parking lot for a minute. Why are you so mean sometimes? What did I ever do to you?"

"Forget it. I'm sorry. Really."

"It's okay," Raven said. "Here. Danny gave this to me. I already took a hit."

She put her palm on mine. For an instant her touch made me tingle, and my hand shook so that I almost dropped the hit of Ecstasy.

• • •

I danced with Raven the rest of the night, frantically and comfortably at the same time. It was a weird feeling, made stranger because I was tripping and horny from the E. Danny edged in a few times, but I wandered away. I didn't want to hold his hand, because I cared about him, and everything I was feeling, stronger all the time now, made it wrong to be near him. I hadn't done anything, but I felt I was betraying him anyway. The worst of it was that I wasn't sure I cared if I did. But more and more I thought I would never be able to love anyone who loved me. The more self-destructive it became, the more I loved Wendy.

And the closer I got to Raven, the more pain I could see

in my future. No more Danny. I'd have to join the Lesbian Collective. I'd already given so much time to Danny, and so much of my inner life to Wendy, I didn't want it to be wasted. Besides, loving Wendy was one thing—it was from a safe distance. Raven was openly gay. How could I know if falling for her was real or only a way to spite Wendy?

I wanted to screw the whole world for making my life so harsh.

"Cary, let's go," Danny said, pulling me off the dance floor at one in the morning.

"I'll take a cab home," I said. "I'm dancing."

I didn't want to let Wendy out of my sight. It suddenly felt very important to cling to her. Otherwise everything would be real—no more safe fantasies.

"You hang out with Raven plenty already," he said. "Spend some time with me."

"You're with your friends. Go do something with them," I said, trying to get back to the dance floor. My feet were humming with the music.

"I want to be with you," he said.

"I want to dance," I said.

He stared at me for a long time. It seemed like minutes, but it was probably only seconds. Then he let go of my arm—dropped it, really.

"Do what you want," he said and walked away.

I had a feeling I should follow him, but suddenly I didn't want to play that game. I wanted to dance with Raven, and also be close to Wendy.

When I got back onto the dance floor and was spinning around Raven, Wendy wiggled in between us, stoned and glassy as usual, but smiling for some reason.

"What happened?" she asked.

"Huh?" I said, acting like I couldn't hear her over the music.

"You and my brother have a fight?" she said in my ear.

"No," I said, trying to move away but unable to. She was a magnet, even when—no especially when—she was being mean.

"I thought maybe you were breaking up or something," she said. I swear her eyes were twinkling.

For a second a sexy thrill ran through me. Was it possible she liked me? This was becoming like one of my fantasies. Why else would she care about Danny and me?

Then she said, "Hey, it's none of my business, but *I* think you should both be seeing other people anyway. I mean it's been what, eleven months or something? What're you going to do, get married or something?"

Now I was really interested, so much that my feet stopped moving. Was this a come-on?

"You wouldn't believe how many girls call the house looking for Danny," Wendy went on. "He could screw a different one every day if he wanted. Right, Raven?"

Raven glared at Wendy while I felt myself shrivel. All my insides were cringing, even though I think I kept a pretty straight face. As Wendy weaved away, Raven leaned close to me. I danced harder, pounding my heels into the wooden floor, wanting the shock waves to ripple through me and rinse me out.

"You're the prettiest girl in school," Raven said. "You know Danny's not sleeping around."

"I don't even care," I said, but not so loudly that she

could hear me. I wanted her to just know, without me saying it. I wanted her to know that I didn't want to be with Danny anymore but that I didn't see any other choice. I couldn't picture myself in a breakup scene unless he did cheat on me. Then at least I could be mad and not feel guilty. Until then, it was easier to fade like an old photo that stays in the family album even after the edges have crumbled and you can't make out the features anymore. You can't tell who it is, or remember who it was, but it stays around.

I spun, letting my skirt whirl into an elegant circle. When I was almost dizzy enough to puke, I stumbled into the corner.

Rad caught me before I slid to the floor, and in another second Raven was holding me under my other arm, leading me to a chair. We all sat down together.

"Feel the energy through your soul / Let the rush take control," Rad said, rubbing behind my ears.

Raven stroked my hand, which was clutching the end of the table. I felt like I was holding onto the earth, trying not to fly off into space. Like I was still spinning, and my head was wobbling on my neck.

"Are you okay?" she asked. She was really concerned and looked like she thought she should be doing something to fix me but didn't know what. I knew she was afraid of touching me too much and maybe making things worse.

"You used to be a victim, now you're not the only one," Rad said.

"Don't pay attention to Wendy. She's just being

bitchy," Raven said. "I'm sorry. I know you don't like me to talk about her, but she shouldn't have said anything like that to you."

"It's not Wendy," I said. "It's me."

"Don't let it bring you down / It's only castles burning," Rad said.

"There are no castles, no fairies, no unicorns, except in paintings or on necklaces," I said.

"What?" Raven said, confused. "I think I should get a cab. You should go home." She paused. "Or you could stay at my house."

"Remember that necklace we saw in the city?" I said.

Rad tried to nudge me closer to Raven, singing, *"There's a girl right next to you / And she's just waiting for something to do."*

"She's not waiting for me," I said to him. "It's not what I want. She's trying to be my friend."

"Wendy is not trying to be your friend," Raven said. Obviously she couldn't hear Rad. Now I knew for sure I really was going crazy. Or I already was crazy.

"Forget it, that's not what I meant," I said to Raven.

"What do you mean?" she asked.

"I just want to go home now," I said. "Alone," I added, looking at Rad.

But he followed me into the cab anyway. He didn't talk, just picked at lint in his belly button, which was fine by me. I didn't need the cabdriver knowing how loony I was. At my house, as Rad strummed his guitar, trailing behind me up the driveway, I stopped and stared at him.

"I don't think you're doing me any good," I said. "Your

little prophecies or platitudes or whatever don't even make that much sense, and I don't feel any clearer, only more confused."

"*In the land of the blind / The one-eyed man is king,*" he said. I heard him, even though I'd shut the door in his face.

Chapter

20

It was a Friday again, and I was at Danny's house, in the basement after sex. I hadn't been in Wendy's room for more than a month because I couldn't bear it. Since New Year's Eve the basement had been my favorite place. I liked to touch the velvet paintings. I wanted to crawl inside them. Sometimes I strummed Wendy's electric guitar, even though I couldn't play, and sometimes Rad joined me, guiding my fingers over the strings or just grooving on the disharmony I made of everything.

I was sitting on a big stool, slowly turning in dreamy circles with pushes of my feet, getting dizzy, when the basement door opened. I froze, but it was only Danny.

"What are you doing down here?" he asked, coming down the stairs.

"Just thinking," I said.

"Thinking about what?"

"Nothing. Not really thinking, I guess. Your mother's paintings are cool."

"They're fucked up," he said, sitting on the concrete floor and looking up at me. "Is something wrong?"

"Why do you keep asking me that? Can't I look at Wile E. Coyote without something being wrong?"

I said it with a smirk, trying to be funny and assuming that would be the end of it. But it wasn't.

"Are you seeing someone else? Do you want to break up?" he asked.

We just had sex, I thought. What more do you want from me? Why don't you just go back to sleep like usual?

But I said, "No, I don't want to break up. I'm just thinking. Just zoning out."

Danny sighed and touched my ankle. His fingers felt like a handcuff. I imagined having to saw through it, or chop off my foot, to be free. I could feel a confrontation coming, and I wanted to avoid that. Audrey Hepburn didn't have to confront things in the movies. The script always had everything work out gently, at the right time, with a minimum of inconvenience for everyone. I wanted to take that path of least resistance, like electricity or water.

"You're distant lately," Danny said. "If it's not another guy, then what? Is something wrong with me? I'm sorry if I don't give you enough attention. I just thought everything was great with us. Don't you know I love you?"

And that is the problem, I thought.

"There is no other guy," I said. "Maybe it's just that at the end of this year we're graduating, and I don't know where we'll go from there."

I was saying whatever came into my head, and I couldn't stop myself. I couldn't lie outright, but I could avoid the truth. I'm tiny. I'm light on my feet. I can sidestep anything.

"You've been hanging around that girl Raven a lot," Danny said. "What has she been telling you? Do you feel bad because you have a boyfriend and she doesn't?"

"Raven has nothing to do with anything," I said, more defensively than I'd intended.

"You know, she's been living here long enough that you don't have to escort her everywhere. She's not the new girl anymore."

"She's my friend. We talk. You know, girl things. I never had a close girlfriend before. It's nice."

"What about your cousin?"

"It's not the same thing." No, it's not, I thought. Raven has better legs. God, I couldn't believe I even thought that.

"I don't want to be in second place," Danny said, very serious.

Now I was scared. What would I do if Danny suddenly broke up with me? Wendy was right. There were tons of girls who would jump on him the second I was out of the way. And then what if no one would go out with me?

"I love you," I said, getting down on the floor and kissing him. I vowed to myself, *again*, to be the best girlfriend ever. It wasn't the New Year's resolution. What mattered was that I didn't want to be left alone.

"I don't know if I want you hanging around Raven anymore," he said, kissing me back.

"What?" I said.

"I'm sorry. It's just since she's been in Babylon everything's different with us. I don't even feel like I know you."

Did you ever? I thought.

"That's not fair. That doesn't even make sense. I don't tell you who you should be friends with."

"Don't be mad. I just want you to talk to *me* more. Why do you need anyone else?"

"That's not the point," I said. "What's going on with you? You never got on my case before. Since when are you so possessive, like you own me or something?"

"I love you, that's all," he said, kissing me.

Faking it was getting harder. I had to go before I collapsed on myself. Suddenly I wished Wendy were around. I mean, she didn't care who I hung around with or what I did. She didn't care about anything. But what a relief that was. It was so much harder knowing people gave a damn what you thought and felt, especially when I didn't feel so strongly about them. It was like my mother wanting to take care of me when I was sick. I wouldn't take care of her—why did she have to bug me?

"Danny," I said, smiling and sweet, "I do love you, and I know you love me. Don't be stupid. There's no reason for me not to be friends with Raven. She likes you. You could be friends with her, too."

Danny sighed. "I'm sorry," he said. "I don't want to pick your friends. I just want to be part of your life, and I don't like feeling shut out."

What a relief! I wouldn't have to chop my ankle off after all. "What time are you picking me up tonight?" I asked.

•   •   •

"*Sometimes I wish that I could stop you from talking / When I hear the silly things that you say,*" Rad said as I got ready to go out that night.

137

Applying eyeliner carefully, I said, "I have to do this my own way. I'll figure it out. But I'm not losing Danny until I'm sure."

"*Tomorrow Wendy,*" Rad said.

"Yeah, maybe," I said. "I have to find out how she feels. But I can work this out."

Rad whistled, almost sadly, but he looked comforted. He didn't even shake or shimmer when he said, "*Surrender, surrender, but don't give yourself away.*"

"I won't," I promised.

Chapter

21

On Saturday night Danny surprised me by driving me into the city for dinner. It was completely unlike him—he never wanted to go farther from home than Phantasie.

"We could just go to a movie," I said.

"I thought you liked the city," he said as we drove along the expressway.

"I do, but you never want to go. I can go into the city any time with my friends."

"I want to be with you. I want to do the things you like to do," he said, smiling at me. He smelled fresh and just shaved, something else he didn't like to do.

Although I smiled back and put my hand on his knee, my stomach felt more rumbly than the truck. I knew Danny was afraid of losing me and he was doing anything he could think of to make me happy. As though that's love. I couldn't even argue with him. I felt chilled, wondering if this would be the last night we spent together and wishing we were at least doing something he wanted to do, so I wouldn't feel so guilty. Was it possible to end this easily and gently, without anyone being hurt?

The cold was worse in the city, as the wind tunneled bitterly past the high buildings and burned our faces. Danny didn't even zip up his leather jacket, but I wrapped my scarf so tightly around my neck and head it almost choked me. I could hardly breathe anyway, so it didn't matter.

We sat in an East Village cafe, eating falafel and listening to a really bad folksinger try to sound like Suzanne Vega—or every other sweet-voiced female singer who could strum a few chords. I barely spoke. Instead I chewed carefully, knowing this couldn't go on forever. I felt like my feet were stuck in quicksand, unable to move forward or back. It was making me sick to not feel anything most of the time except emptiness. I could cope with not having a boyfriend. But I couldn't cope with not having Wendy.

"I was thinking that this summer we could go visit my cousins in North Carolina," Danny said.

"Uh-huh, maybe," I said. The time to tell him wasn't right yet.

I have to find a way to approach Wendy, I thought. Gulping at my beer, I imagined what would happen if—when—she rejected me. I wouldn't be able to love anyone ever again. If I couldn't have this one thing I wanted, what would be the point? If I couldn't love Danny and I couldn't have Wendy, that was it. I couldn't be gay—there, I finally thought it—and I couldn't be straight. There wouldn't be anyone, anywhere, for me. Not even Raven. I wasn't anything like her ex, Kelly. I was pathetic.

"Do you want another beer?" Danny asked.

I want a life, I thought.

I could hide myself away and write poems, like Emily

Dickinson. Then people could say, she always was weird, watching all those old movies and dressing like a dead movie star.

• • •

After dinner we drove to Coney Island and walked on the boardwalk, even though the wind coming off the ocean was like ice in motion. Danny held me close, and I wrapped both my arms around him so our hips bumped when we walked. My heels clicked on the wooden slats. Coney Island is scary at night, especially in the off-season. All the rides are closed, and everywhere gangs of kids are drinking forty-ounce bottles of beer and smoking pot and crack and cigarettes. I was terrified every time we passed by the tough-looking freaks and mean-looking kids, but it was better to be scared of them than to feel safe with Danny. I could run from other people, but I couldn't run from myself.

Danny kissed me next to the Cyclone, and someone whistled.

"Let's go home," I said.

A couple was making out on the hood of Danny's truck, and they glared at us as we got in and started the engine. Great, I thought as they separated and got down. Another romance I've fucked up.

• • •

Back at the house Danny cleared a space on the couch, pushing newspapers onto the floor and piling some sweaters and other dirty clothes into pillows. We kissed for a while with the TV's blue light shimmering on us and making long shadows on the wall. During a rerun of *Quantum Leap* on the sci-fi channel, Danny fell asleep in the nest of smelly laundry, and I slid off the couch to the floor. Just as I wondered if Wendy was home, upstairs sleeping, or with one of her boyfriends, a key turned in the lock and she stumbled in. Her eyes swept past me, and she teetered into the kitchen, falling against the wall and then pushing off again. I followed her as she took the bottle of vodka from the ironing board and eased her way carefully into the basement. She collapsed by her guitar, almost knocking it off its stand, and took a drink from the bottle.

"Are you okay?" I asked, sitting next to her, feeling my heart beat so fast it was practically out of my chest.

"Hey, what's up?" she said, just noticing me.

I wiped the vodka dribbling down her chin. Her skin was soft, like the velvet paintings on the wall. She wasn't wearing a bra, and her nipples were hard from the cold. I wondered where her coat was.

"I love you," I said.

"Man, the club was wild tonight!" she said, leaning into me.

Had she heard me? I wondered. I couldn't say it again. I didn't have the strength. My whole body was throbbing and my mind was swimming through jellied thoughts, trying to figure out if this was it, if this was my chance, if this was the right time.

"What should I say?" I asked Rad, who was tuning Wendy's guitar to match his own.

"Punk rock girl, give me a chance," he suggested.

"What should I do?" I asked, not really listening to him anyway. He didn't know any more than I did.

"Practice what you preach," he said.

Wendy's eyes were drooping shut, and I knew I didn't

have much time. But Rad was right. I couldn't keep living in this dream world. No matter what happened, I needed closure, or something. Even if it meant ruining my life.

So I did it. I kissed her on the lips. She didn't move away. She leaned in closer, smelling like booze and pot and cigarette smoke. The vodka bottle dropped sideways and rolled away, leaving a trail of clear stink and finally stopping against the side of the spool table. I kissed Wendy again, and she opened her mouth. Frantically, I touched her everywhere, hardly noticing that she didn't touch me back. She only clutched at my hair. Kissing her, I felt like I was kissing my own spirit and giving it life. Nothing radiated from her, not even desire really, but she was willing, and I knew I had enough for both of us. At least she wasn't pushing me away, which I took to be a good sign.

"This is hard for me, too," I said, thinking maybe she was embarrassed to respond. Deep down I knew she was just drunk, but when she reached between my legs, I thought, this is really it. She wants me. She needs me, too.

Chapter

22

I BARELY SLEPT THAT NIGHT. I KEPT WAKING UP, SMILING, thinking of Wendy. Then Sunday morning I could hardly keep my eyes open. I was still smiling, but now I couldn't get Danny off my mind. I knew I had to tell him about me and Wendy, if she hadn't already. Finally, at two in the afternoon my mother knocked on my bedroom door. Staring dreamily up at the unicorn painting, I rubbed my hands over my face.

"Cary, your friend Raven's here. Were you supposed to do something together?" my mother called through the door.

Oh God! Raven! I couldn't deal with her right now. My head felt heavy, and it was all I could do to push myself out of bed and into a pale yellow cardigan and black pants. When I went into the kitchen, Raven was sipping coffee. She smiled at me.

"Late night?" she asked, innocence and beauty. I wanted to tell her, but her cheeks were too flushed with rosy anticipation of a day ice skating at Argyle Lake.

"I can't go skating with you today," I said carefully.

"There's something I have to do that's really important. I'm sorry."

"Hey, no big deal. We'll do it after school or next weekend or something," she said, still sitting at the kitchen table, still sipping from her cup.

"Would you mind going now?" I said.

"Yeah, I'm just warming up a little—"

"I'm sorry, I can't explain now, but I need you to go, now." I turned away so I wouldn't see if she looked hurt.

"Sure" was all she said as she zipped up her coat and left.

• • •

A few hours later I was at Danny's house, feeling funny sitting in his bedroom. The first thing he tried to do was lean over me and put his tongue in my mouth.

After kissing me he said, "I'm so glad you're here. It would've been okay for you to go skating with your friend. I decided it's okay whoever you're friends with. But I'm glad you're here. I love you. You're so beautiful."

Oh my God, I thought, shrinking away. How could I do this? Maybe I should wait until Wendy was home and we could do it together.

"When's Wendy coming back?" I asked. Just saying her name gave me chills. My fingertips still had green stains on them from touching her hair last night. I could remember every breath I took. She was printed on my mind, and her shadow was etched over my body.

"She went with my mother to the store or something. I don't know. What does it matter? I'm glad we're together," Danny said. He tried to kiss me again, and I pushed him gently away.

"What?" he asked.

"Danny, I want to tell you first that I never lied about loving you. I care about you very much, which is why this is very hard. I can't put it off anymore. If you're going to be mad, I'll understand, just please only be mad at me. I started it . . ."

"You did sleep with another guy! There *is* someone else! I knew it! You lied to me!"

"I didn't," I said, putting my hand on Danny's knee. He dropped his head and his long, black, shiny hair fell over his face. I was glad not to be able to see his eyes.

"I mean, there isn't another guy," I said slowly. Finally, I blurted, "I love Wendy."

"Excuse me?" Danny said, looking at me and almost laughing. "Are you totally psycho? I mean if you want to have a fight, let's fight, but what's Wendy got to do with it?"

"Danny, I had sex with her. I'm in love. I've been in love with her for a while. I've just been trying not to be, because I care about you, and because I was scared . . ."

Danny got off the bed and went to his dresser, lighting a cigarette. His corduroys hung low on his hips, exposing the band of his underwear. His shirt, an old bowling shirt with *Kurt* in red script over the chest, hung open. I approached him and placed my hand against the wiry hair on his chest.

"I'm sorry," I said. "I know it's a lot to hear at once. No one else knows, so you don't have to feel embarrassed—"

"You're crazy, you know that?" Danny said, slapping my hand away. "But I don't know why you have to bring my sister into this. My sister! That's really sick."

146

"Danny, I—"

"Just get out. Go home."

"Maybe I should wait for Wendy, so we can—"

"*I'll* talk to Wendy," he said. "I think you need help."

• • •

I couldn't go home, so I went to Raven's house. Up in her room I handed her tacks as she rearranged the posters on her wall.

"So," I said, "you still haven't gotten your room just right?" I tried to sound light and airy and carefree, even though I felt like sticking a tack into my palm.

"That's practically the first thing you've said since you've been here," she said. "If you're going to stay for dinner, you better improve your conversation skills, or my mother will think you're weird."

"Everyone else does," I whispered.

"What?" she said, getting down off the chair. She grabbed my hand and stared at me.

My face felt tight. I didn't want to tell her—I wanted to tell her even less than I'd wanted to tell Danny, which surprised me. Her hair was pulled back into a ponytail, and her eyes were done up with that pretty lavender eyeshadow, but all I could see were Wendy's purple eyebrows and puckered lips.

"I slept with Wendy," I blurted.

Raven sank to the edge of the bed and teetered until I put my hand on her shoulder to stop her from rocking. I already felt sick to my stomach.

"Please be happy for me. You're the only one I could tell."

"I'm glad you got what you wanted," she said.

147

"I think everything'll work out now," I said. "You're not mad at me, are you?" But I knew she was.

"Does Danny know?"

"I told him. He's freaking out. He doesn't believe me, but I guess after he talks to Wendy, we'll start to deal with it. Somehow."

"How could you do this to me?" Raven said then, looking up at me with wet eyes.

Suddenly I was angry, maybe because I couldn't handle being sad, not when what I wanted for so long was now within reach.

"Do this to you?" I said. "I did this for me! Why is everything I do supposed to be about someone else?"

"Didn't you know how I felt about you?" Raven demanded.

"We're friends," I said. "You never said anything else."

"So you're saying you didn't know? I knew you were gay. I've known since I first met you. I didn't push you, I waited, I was so fucking patient, and you go and have sex with that, that *bitch!* She's a fucking bitch, and she doesn't give a shit about anyone but herself. Maybe you deserve each other!"

I was in shock. I'd never heard Raven even raise her voice before, and here she was, cursing and screaming at me. My mind started to go into shutdown. I didn't want to crash, not here, not now. Wasn't it enough that I'd just had sex with a girl last night? With my boyfriend's sister, no less? Now I had to deal with this? Uh-uh.

"I'm leaving. Don't ever talk to me again," I said.

Raven let me go without a word, and I avoided Adam

on the stairs, brushing past before he could attack me with those angry, twelve-year-old, wannabe-the-big-brother eyes. I walked home in the cold without my coat. I'd left it on Raven's floor. When I got home, my hands were frozen and chapped. I could barely answer the phone when it rang.

"So you want to tell me what's going on?" Danny said.

"Did you talk to Wendy?" I asked.

"She said it was all a fantasy, in your head. God, I didn't know you were so fucked up. Is it drugs? Have you been partying too hard? Were you high this afternoon?"

"Excuse me?" I said, shaking my head and feeling it grow hot while the rest of me chilled all the way through. "She said what?"

"She said it never happened, but she sees you looking at her all the time, and she should have known you'd make up something crazy like this. How could you?" Danny said.

"Let me talk to her," I said.

"She's out," Danny said. "With a guy. God, how could you say that about my sister? How many people have you told?"

"None. But I'm not lying. Why would I lie about something like that?"

"I don't know, that's what I'm asking you," Danny said. "Were you just trying to make me mad?"

"Wendy and I had sex last night. After you went to sleep."

"So now you're calling my sister a liar, too? Do you think I don't know her a little better than that? She may be a pain in the ass, but she wouldn't lie to me. I didn't think you would, either, but God, we're talking about my sister here!"

"I don't know what to say," I said, and it was true. I'd never expected this. I thought maybe Wendy would beg Danny not to tell their parents. At worst, I thought she might say we couldn't ever do it again, that she couldn't handle it. I never expected her to call me a psycho and a liar. Next thing you knew, she'd be going on *Ricki Lake* or something. Without saying anything else, I hung up the phone and walked quietly upstairs to my room, trying not to feel anything. When I got there and saw the unicorn painting where I used to hide my Wendy collection, I exploded. I started crying, and I pulled the painting off the wall so hard the screw it had been hanging from was yanked out, and plaster spilled from the hole onto my pillow.

As I pounded at the glass covering the painting, not caring about the biting cuts on my knuckles, Rad tried to pull me back.

"*Beneath the stain of time / The feeling disappears,*" he said.

"No, let me go!" I screamed. "How could she?"

"*She's just a devil woman / With evil on her mind,*" he said, trying to comfort me but making me feel worse.

I dug my nails into the exposed paper of the painting, bleeding on it as I tore. "Danny doesn't even believe me now. He thinks I'm crazy!"

"*And the words ate into his brain . . .*"

"Oh, shut up!" I said, pushing Rad away. He fell against his guitar, and I heard the splintering of wood. I

150

froze. "Oh God, I'm sorry. I don't know what I'm doing. Are you okay? Is your guitar . . . I don't believe this is happening to me," I said, sinking to the floor next to Rad. The guitar was cracked a little but not broken, thankfully. I put my arm around him.

"Thank God you're here," I said. "Help me. It's all over, isn't it? The one person who believes me is Raven, and she hates me now. What am I going to do? It's over. I wish I was dead."

I started to cry as Rad picked bits of glass out of my knuckles. My stomach was twisted, and I felt a sharp pain in my ribs and shoulder as I gasped for air. It was hard to cry with so much going on. I didn't know what to cry about first. That it was over with Danny, that I meant nothing to Wendy, that Raven would never speak to me again, that Wendy would spread it around school that I was a psycho-dyke and that no one would be there to defend me, that . . .

"Just a little patience," Rad said.

"I don't think I can stand it. I can't deal with hurting this bad," I cried.

"Everybody hurts sometimes," he said, stroking me until I was only sobbing and I could breathe at least.

I still wanted to die, but I got up, shakily grabbed my wastebasket, and started cleaning up the mess on my bed. Gradually, I stopped crying. Cope, cope, cope, I thought. I can cope.

"So like it or not, you will have to be free," Rad said.

That was the scariest thing anyone ever said to me, so I just kept dropping shards of glass and scraps of unicorn into the garbage. And telling myself, I will cope.

I COULDN'T GO TO SCHOOL THAT WEEK. I COULDN'T FACE anyone. I didn't even eat. I just stared at the ceiling. I yelled at my mother for trying to empty my garbage can. I needed to be able to look at the broken remains of my unicorn and try to remember how happy I'd felt with Wendy, and even with Danny. But it was hard. I couldn't remember how either of them smelled, even. It was like my mind was blank. I was totally empty, and no one, not even Rad, could fill me up again.

"You're losing weight again," he said to me at one point in my blankness. *"Did you ever wonder who you're losing it for?"*

I only rolled off the bed and under it, breathing in dust.

• • •

Friday I got out of bed and put on the strapless black dress I'd worn on New Year's Eve. I fastened my pearls around my neck with shaky hands and applied eyeliner and red lipstick. My mother came in as I was brushing my hair for the hundredth time, staring into the mirror.

"You're up," she said.

I nodded.

"You're not going out tonight," she said. "You've been sick all week."

"I'm better now," I said.

My father came in behind my mother. "You're not better. Tomorrow you're going to the doctor."

"I've been depressed, that's all," I said. "I have to go out tonight. There's something I have to do."

"Cary!" my mother shouted as I slipped between my parents.

When the cab came, my parents were together on the couch in the living room, shaking their heads and whispering. I guess they felt like they should be "parental," but they didn't know what to say. They didn't know what to do with me, and I didn't blame them—how could they understand?

●　●　●

I ate dinner by myself at Friendly's, not caring that people were looking at me funny, especially when I started crying over the green sprinkles on my ice cream sundae. I almost went home, but I told myself, I have to take responsibility. More important, I need some kind of closure. I need to hear it from Wendy herself. So at eleven o'clock I walked through the front door of Phantasie for the first time ever without having a drink first, or a hit of E, or anything to help me cope. I was testing my strength. I was also, I knew in my heart, still feeling optimistic. I couldn't believe it was all over. No matter how many thousands of times I'd chanted it to myself, I *couldn't* cope. But I wasn't going to freak out until it was really over.

Wendy was dancing, and as I glided toward her, it was like my feet weren't even touching the floor. For a second I thought I was going to cry, remembering all the time I'd spent here, with Danny and, later, Raven too. Were they here tonight? I was afraid to look.

Everyone must have known, because a path was cleared for me. The Lesbian Collective, who had been ignoring me for a while, now wandered onto the dance floor behind Wendy, and I could almost see concern in their faces. I don't know why. It wasn't like I had ever treated them like people. Why should they care about me? Why should anyone? Except Wendy.

She stopped dancing when I was right in front of her.

"Do you know how much you've hurt me?" I yelled over the music.

She waved me away.

I could tell she was really high and hardly even seeing me. I grabbed her arm. When she looked in my direction, I lightened my grip and started to cry.

"I love you," I said. "Doesn't that mean anything to you?"

"I don't know what you're talking about," she said, moving away.

I followed her.

"Cary, stop," someone said. It was Raven. "Forget about her."

But I couldn't stop. I followed Wendy as she went outside.

"Go away!" she yelled at me. People waiting on line to get in stared. "Leave me alone, you crazy bitch!"

And she started running, wobbling on her high heels past the parking lot.

Chapter

24

SATURDAY MORNING I LOCKED MYSELF IN MY FATHER'S STUDY, bleary from too little sleep. My jaw ached from grinding my teeth during the few times I had dozed off. With my headphones on so I wouldn't hear if my parents knocked on the door, I stared at a blank page in my notebook, trying to think of how to tell Wendy how much I loved her. When I finally started to write, it sounded too pathetic. I decided instead to call her.

I ran my hands through my hair, which was all greasy tangles, clumped and frazzle-shaped from old hairspray. My lips were dry. I moved to the sofa, by the phone. Closing my eyes, I could feel Wendy's elbows sharp against me. I picked up the phone.

No one answered. I kept calling, and still no one answered, not all day. I wondered if Wendy was in her room, smoking a joint and stroking her cat, maybe thinking of me. She couldn't hate me. But if she did, that was maybe okay, so long as she was thinking of me.

• • •

On Sunday Mr. Waterman answered the phone.

"Hi, is Wendy there?" I asked, bright and, I hoped, casual.

"No, she's not," he said. His voice was gruff but choked. Wendy must have told him, I thought.

I tried again a half hour later. This time Danny answered, and he recognized my voice. "Don't call here again" was all he said. Not even hello first.

I called again a half hour later. Danny hung up on me.

After three more tries, I had some lunch. Nibbling on the crust of a thick piece of sourdough bread, I wondered if Wendy was grounded. Why else wouldn't they let me talk to her? My mother came into the kitchen with a vase and some flowers, and I watched her out of the corner of my eye, thinking, had the Watermans called her? If they know about me and Wendy, does my mother know, too?

I decided no. She was too calm, and my father was at the country club playing cards. If they knew, he'd be home, and we'd all be sitting in the living room having a deep discussion or something. I gently placed my dish in the sink and slinked out of the kitchen. Eventually I'd have to tell them, but I wanted to settle things with Wendy first.

I felt better as I showered, rubbing my skin smooth with a loofah. When I rubbed my hands over my body, I felt Wendy's body under my hands. My eyes shut, I let my fingers travel over the knobby curve of her spine, and I could smell her, woodsy, elfin. The taste of her teeth was in my mouth.

I took my time putting on makeup and curling my little

bangs under. I wore long, leather gloves with my leopard jacket and dark glasses. Sneaking out the side door so my mother wouldn't notice that I wasn't dressed warmly enough, I headed toward Wendy's. If they wouldn't let me in, I'd stand on the sidewalk and shout. I'd throw pebbles from the driveway at Wendy's window.

The Waterman house was dark, shadowy cold, shaded in winter grays. Forgetting the broken top step, I stepped on it and sank in. My ankles were too cold to feel pain, although I knew I'd scratched myself badly pulling my foot out of the old wood. Knocking, I almost expected my knuckles to crack, brittle from the cold, which my gloves hadn't kept out.

Danny answered the door. I put my foot in it so he couldn't shut it.

"I know you're upset, Danny, but just let me talk to her. If we all talk about it—"

"Wendy left," he said.

"When's she coming back?" I asked.

"She *left*," he said, kicking at my foot, trying to get it out of the way. "We don't know where she is. We don't know anything. Thanks a lot."

"What are you talking about?"

"She ran away."

"Not because of me!"

"No. My father thinks she might be pregnant. But you didn't help, making up stories. She left a note. She said she was getting married, and that she wasn't a dyke, no matter what you said. What did you say to her at Phantasie?"

"What do you mean, married? To who? Let me see the note. Please?"

"If you and Wendy were as close as you say, you should know, right?" Danny said.

He got my foot out of the way with one last kick at my toes and slammed the door so hard the porch shook.

"This is bullshit!" I yelled. "You're making it all up! Where's Wendy? Wendy! Wendy, come out and talk to me!"

• • •

My mother had to come get me when I wouldn't leave the Watermans'. "Breakups happen," she said, looking more embarrassed than concerned as she loaded me, stiff, into the car. "It's no reason to throw a tantrum."

I had kicked at the door so long and hard, the toes of my shoes were crushed in.

My mother continued, "It's not as though Danny's the only boy in town. And soon you'll be away at school. It was bound to happen sooner or later."

So she didn't know anything really.

"I don't care about Danny," I said, barely moving my lips. They were cracked and chapped.

My mother chuckled. "It didn't seem that way to me," she said.

"It's not funny!" I said. "You don't get it at all!"

In the garage she wiped at the mascara stains on my cheeks, and pulled me into a hug. The gearshift poked my stomach, hurting. "You're not the only one to go through this," she said. "We all do."

"Just forget it!" I said, pushing her away. "You don't understand!"

I ran inside, up to my room, kicked off my shoes,

and threw myself under my covers, still dressed. My feet felt swollen and my toes throbbed as they thawed. When I started crying, I couldn't stop. Everything was ruined, everything was over. I'd fucked everything up so bad.

Chapter

25

I WANDERED THROUGH THE NEXT SEVERAL DAYS, FORCING myself to exist and spending my lunches on the pay phone, dialing the Watermans' number, hoping Wendy would answer, hoping she had come back. It was all over school that she'd run away with the guy with the dragon tattoo. I was nothing.

Something inside told me I should let go—she'd dumped me, first by lying and then by disappearing. But if I let go, I didn't know how far I might fall. Imagining Wendy's fatigue-green fingernails against my thighs kept me sane. That, and thinking she'd come back to me. If I couldn't have had sex with her in the basement without being in love, how could she? Dragon-guy wasn't right for her, even if it was true she was pregnant. Poor Wendy.

I wish she had come to me about her problems. She didn't have to run away. I would've helped her. I guess she was afraid to let anyone see her upset.

No one sat in Wendy's seat in calculus. And no one came *near* me. I erected a wall for myself, isolated from

Danny's sneers and the glances of anyone else who might care. Raven didn't even try to get close to me. Jen was skiing with her parents in Aspen, which was a relief. I wasn't looking forward to her return, even if she might be the only one who would believe me but not judge me.

But in a way, it didn't matter to me that I couldn't tell anyone my side. I just wanted Wendy back. I counted the moments until she'd appear, wanting me, apologizing, crying on my shoulder. Then forever would begin.

• • •

I was at Argyle Lake after school, sitting on a chipped bench and staring at the lumpy ice and the junior high hockey players. I recognized Raven's brother, Adam. He skated pretty well for a kid from Texas. As he skimmed past, he raised a hand and nodded. I guess now that he had his own friends, he didn't have time to bother with me and didn't care anymore if I made his sister cry. Unless maybe I hadn't made her cry this time. Maybe even Raven had given up on me.

"Hey," said a voice. Danny's.

"Hey," I said, surprised to see him standing there, his long hair blowing in the crisp wind, swirling around his head.

"Have you heard something?" I asked, standing up and feeling light. "Wendy's back?"

Danny's face got hard. "No. I just came by because, well your mother said you were here, and I thought . . . I just want you to tell me the truth. Why Wendy? What'd she do to you? Why did you have to make up that stupid story, and keep telling lies? I only want to understand. I

161

don't want to hate you. Maybe if you explain . . . It's hard enough for me, with Wendy taking off. I don't want to lose you, too."

"Danny," I said, "I swear I told you the truth. But I wasn't trying to hurt you. I thought Wendy loved me, too. I didn't force her. She could've said no, and I would have been embarrassed, but I wouldn't have pushed her. I guess you could say I seduced her, but I'm not a slut. I've been in love with her for—"

"God!" Danny shouted. "What is *wrong* with you? I came here to give you a chance to apologize for what you did, for lying like that. Can't you give it up already?"

"No, I can't give it up!" I yelled back. "Do you know how much I cared about her? It's not easy for me. I'm hurt, too, you know!"

"You're not even sorry, are you?" Danny shouted, getting so close I cringed, afraid he was going to hit me.

"I'm sorry for everything. I never wanted anyone hurt. I wanted everyone to be happy," I said, knowing how stupid that sounded. But it was true.

"I can't even talk to you. You are dead to me," Danny said. "I can't believe I actually slept with you! I can't believe I said I loved you. Excuse me, I have to go scrub my mouth out and wash my dick.

"You fucking bitch," he said as he hurried away.

I didn't cringe this time, but my head hurt. I was so upset with him for reminding me again that Wendy had betrayed me and that it was probably over forever. Oh God, I thought, how can this be happening to me? Dropping my head into my hands, I squeezed my eyes shut, trying to remember Wendy in a way that was good.

· · ·

"How long are you going to stay here? You can't bring her back."

It was Raven, crouching next to me on the ground where I was forcing my cold fingers to braid pine needles into rings. They were scattered on the frosty ground around me. Raven picked up one of the twisted circles.

"It's not diamonds, but it's a look," she said.

"It's not funny," I said.

"I know," she said, putting an arm around me.

I picked up another pine needle and tried to make it bend into a loop, but it broke before I could fasten it. That was when I started to cry. I cried for a long time, pulling at the rings I'd made and breaking them all. Raven looked like a woodland urchin from some futuristic movie, her fluffy pimp-coat matted with my tears and prickly with broken pine needles. She didn't seem to care. She just kept holding me until I stopped crying.

"The really sad thing," I said, swallowing hard, "is that I'm not sure anymore if I even really loved her. It was all in my head.

"Oh God," I said, sobbing again. "I *did* use her! I used her to work out my own head. I just expected her to say no, and then I would go on with Danny, pretending I loved him. I did love him, I did!"

"It's okay," Raven said.

"It'll never be okay. No one will ever love me. I've ruined everything. Danny hates me, Wendy's gone, my parents will probably hate me when they find out. I have to tell them something, I don't know what Jen is going to say, she probably hates me, you hate me . . ."

"I love you," Raven said.

I looked at her and I knew it was true. And God help me, as bad as I felt, I actually gave a shit. I wanted her to love me, even if I didn't deserve it. I wanted to stop waiting for Wendy to come back. I wanted to believe that loving someone else wouldn't mean that I'd wasted myself on Wendy, that my feelings hadn't been real.

"Here," Raven said, taking a small box from her pocket. When I didn't open it right away, she said, "It's okay if you don't want it. I saved the receipt. I can take it back. I just want to make you happy. Please open it."

So I did. Inside, resting softly on a square of cotton, was a silver unicorn pendant. It was the one we'd seen on St. Marks Place when we were shopping in the city on Christmas Eve.

Stroking it, I said, "Are you sure? It's going to take me time to get over Wendy, and I don't know what will happen if she comes back. I don't know how I'll handle it."

Raven waved her hand and shook her head. "Enough," she said. "Nothing happens overnight. But now you know how I feel about you. I'll care about you no matter what."

I nodded.

Raven took my hand and lifted me from the ground. I held the charm tightly in my hand, drawing life from it even as its tiny horn pinched my skin.

"Let's at least get out of the cold. We can talk," Raven said. Then she added, "If it's okay . . ."

"Yeah, it's okay," I said.

• • •

Rad walked with us to the parking lot. I could hardly see him. The harder I held Raven with one hand and the

164

unicorn with the other, the more he seemed to disappear. His goatee blinked away, then his chin. His guitar was just a shadow.

But he was smiling when he said, *"Look at the state I'm in."*

"Excuse me for just a second," I said to Raven. She looked worried, but she let me go back, behind the trees, by myself.

"What's happening to you, Rad?" I asked.

"I am ashes, I am Jesus, I am precious," he said so softly his voice was almost part of the wind.

Now his high-tops were gone, and his skinny legs. He was floating.

"You're leaving?" I asked. "How can you leave? What will I have left? Who will I talk to?"

"If you see the wonder of a fairy tale / You can take the future even if you fail."

He was almost gone.

"Where will you go?" I asked, trying to hold on to him, but there was nothing to grab. His pale blond hair was barely a memory.

"I'm gonna go where it's always cloudy," he said, smiling.

"I'm not cloudy enough for you anymore?" I said, afraid of knowing the answer, knowing I might start to be happy now. I hoped if I could keep him talking, Rad wouldn't go.

"I'm just a jukebox hero," he said. All that was left were his blue eyes, deep and soft, and his wide mouth.

"No!" I said desperately. "I'm not ready! It's not over yet. I can't deal by myself. You're the only one . . ."

But I couldn't see him anymore. The faint twang of

guitar strings hung in the air with Rad's last words to me, *"Feet on ground, heart in hand / Facing forward, be yourself."*

• • •

"Cary, are you okay?" Raven yelled from the parking lot.

I looked at the silver unicorn in my hand and the reddish impression it left in my palm.

"I think so," I said. "I'm coming."

Then I whispered to her, even though she was too far away to hear, "I like you, too." Maybe even love you.

Shelley Stoehr is a dance teacher and massage therapist. She is also the author of the acclaimed *Crosses, Weird on the Outside,* and *Wannabe.* Shelley lives in Los Angeles.